ONE DEADLY SOUK

MX Publishing

Other books in the CODE NAME DELTA series:

The Quadrille

Red Goliath

The Caribbean Sedition

The Magdalena Gambit

Killing for Profit

Man on Target

The Impostor

A New Kind of War

King of the Slaughtermen

A Honey Smeared Trap

To Know is to Die

The Circumstantial Hitman

The Poisonous Hand

Dead Dog Won't Bite

THE SECRET FILE OF PATRICK COONAN

ONE DEADLY SOUK

Oscar Ortiz

MX Publishing

Book #3 in the CODE NAME DELTA series

ONE DEADLY SOUK

Copyright © 2024 by Oscar F. Ortiz

MX Publishing
**335 Princess Park Manor, Royal Drive,
London, N11 3GX, United Kingdom**

Paperback ISBN: 978-1-80424-472-2
eBook PDF ISBN: 978-1-80424-474-6
eBook ePub ISBN: 978-1-80424-473-9

*To my son Alex Francisco,
my dear 'Big Guy'*

Praise for One Deadly Souk

AWARDED 3 STARS BY THE ONLINE BOOK CLUB

"An engaging and descriptive narration, with the perfect balance between telling and showing that creates vivid imagery and brings the complex geo-political situation to life with a character-driven plot. Recommended for readers who like action and adventure novels. Fans of Ian Fleming's James Bond will certainly appreciate this novel."

— **Patel Khushi Manishbhai**
Reviewer for The Online Book Club

A DANGEROUS & COMPLEX MISSION

"The adventures continue for Patrick Coonan, but they are becoming more and more dangerous with every new assignment he is handed by his chief and, above all, extremely complicated! Agent Delta's current mission in Colombia is about (but not limited to) engaging an old enemy from the Cold War, while simultaneously being wary of his present allies – allies who can turn and will become formidable adversaries at any given moment... This is what our favorite eliminator discovers in this joint mission with a maverick agent from the OCF's Moscow Bureau, where he will have to put his neck on the line to unravel very complex situations!"

— **Renan Bourgeat**
Agent Delta's #1 French fan, and Amazon reviewer

HOOKED UNTIL THE VERY END

"Whoever reads a line of One Deadly Souk *runs the risk of*

getting so hooked on its plot that he or she will not be able to put it down until the very end. Brandishing a sui generis narrative, Oscar Ortiz takes us on a vertiginous journey into the bowels of the most sophisticated counterespionage. Without lyricism, with the crudeness of a fiction that skirts the limits of reality and an extraordinary knowledge of weapons, Ortiz steers us through a labyrinth of mixed emotions that inexorably leads to an unexpected outcome."

— **Ernesto Morales Alpízar**
Author of Terror in Miami

LIKE THE VERY BEST OF SPILLANE & HAMMETT

"In this day and age, is hard to believe that there are still those who write Mike Hammer-style paperback espionage novels. Perhaps that's why I enjoyed reading One Deadly Souk so much. To my surprise, besides the literary déjà vu, I discovered that this book has the same ingredients as a Tom Clancy bestseller; only fewer pages and a lot more punch. In fact, it reads in one sitting, like the best of Mickey Spillane, or those of Dashiell Hammett. It is so well written, so scenically strung together, that, instead of a novel, it reads more like a movie script that didn't make it to the screen."

— **Manuel C. Díaz**
Book critic of El Nuevo Herald

AN ENGAGING READ

"The character development in this book is outstanding. Each character is unique. A truly engaging read!

— **Sandre Lamar**
Member of The Online Book Club

"Sometimes one must pact with the devil to avoid a greater evil."

TABLE OF CONTENTS

FOREWORD

(An introduction to The Secret File of Patrick Coonan)

In recent times, the cinematic James Bond has been converted into a "catwalk muscleman" bearing an asphalt face and a propensity for melancholy. To escape from this new "politically correct" version of the character, incapable of being seductive and without any trace of the model developed by Ian Fleming in his novels, there still are a few options available. The most obvious one is to review Fleming's books or the films starring Sean Connery and his most popular successors. Another option is the pulp narrative alternative to 007, currently well-served by the prolific Cuban American writer Oscar Ortiz. This is the series *Code Name Delta*, starring Patrick Coonan, a U.S. Rangers' sniper transformed into a clandestine operator for the Quadrille —the sharp counterintelligence unit created by Ret. Special Forces Col. Marlon Berkowitz to safeguard America from all threats. Always with the protracted shadow of the Cold War as the background, which also served as the main setting in the first Bond book written by Fleming. Ortiz's virtues as a novelist can be well-appreciated in all his Patrick Coonan adventures: a concise, direct prose, halfway between the noir mystery genre and the spy thriller; utmost erudition in the different topics dealt with, where one perceives a thorough work of research and the offering to the reader of varied plots that combine investigation, violent death, sexuality, and an uncomfortable background of moral sordidness.

Josep Ferran Valls
Valencia, Spain - Oct. 2022

DRAMATIS PERSONAE

AHMED
A mysterious guerrilla commander of Muslim origin, who has been sighted meeting with Yuri Pavenko and The Scorpion at the Club Terraza in Cali, Colombia.

ALEDO (Margot)
CI5's chief of staff; she also oversees the Shared Archives Department. Mrs. Aledo serves as Col. Berkowitz's right hand in administration matters within headquarters.

ARTEAGA (Carlos Rafael)
Alias *El Alacrán* (The Scorpion). A dangerous Colombian drug trafficker. He owns the Club Terraza — a salsa nightclub in the suburb of Juanchito, in Cali, Colombia.

BERKOWITZ (Marlon)
A.k.a. the Colonel. A former member of the U.S. Special Forces, and Vietnam War veteran, he is the founder and director of operations of the Quadrille. Coonan's chief. Col. Berkowitz is the head of CI5.

CEDEÑO (Bartolo)
General of the Colombian Army in charge of capturing guerrillas and major drug dealers, he is the fearless leader of the *Bloque de Búsqyeda* (BdB), also known as the Search Bloc.

COONAN (Patrick)
He is Col. Berkowitz's best eliminator; also, one of his most loyal followers who deserves all his trust. Protagonist of this series. His code name is Delta.

FELDMAN (Arnold)
General Director of the Organized Crime Force (OCF). A man of intrigue and great influence in Washington political circles.

FITTS (Jessica)
Intelligence analyst hired by the Colonel to join the new Quadrille, now operating as CI5. She is also Pat's new partner. Her code name is Phi.

LONG (Mortimer)
An OCF special agent stationed at the Moscow Bureau, and the man who

Director Feldman counts on to catch Yuri Pavenko and put him behind bars.

PAVENKO (Yuri)
Dangerous black-market trafficker of weapons of mass destruction. He is a former Soviet KGB nuclear saboteur.

TETRIAK (Nina)
Alias Nina the Gunslinger, Pavenko's young protégé. She is also his right hand in the weapons trafficking business and his main enforcer.

TILSON (Alfred)
Second in the command hierarchy of the old Quadrille, also the Colonel's confidant and Pat's trainer. In the new CI5 he serves as a liaison officer between the Colonel and Director Feldman.

ZAMBRANO LORA (César)
General Cedeño's personal assistant. He also serves as a liaison between the Search Bloc and the OCF.

A GHOST FROM THE PAST

Part One

*P*rologue

In times of the Cold War, we existed only as a unit of ill-fated characters *unofficially* known as the Quadrille. I emphasize "unofficially" because, although our crew was shaped and run following the pattern and directive of the U.S. government's Department of Defense, the Quadrille from that epoch was never recognized as an "official agency" by its Washington administrators; neither was the budget that financed all the training and sophisticated scaffolding that my boss had to assemble to sustain its complex infrastructure. Nothing Col. Marlon Berkowitz did was ever documented. All about our group was surreptitious, as were the identities and positions occupied by the men and women who closed our ranks.

From the beginning of its lethal actions (the secret missions that were carried out against all odds), the Quadrille was used to fight the saboteurs of the Soviet Bloc who made up the Atomic Fang Division of the former KGB and, incidentally, any other enemy operatives sent to do harm on American soil. The men and women who made up the first line of clandestine defense of the American Union were tagged as "eliminators," professional killers specially trained by Alfred Tilson, a CIA master assassin imported from The Company's Moscow Section, to hunt down the big guns of the opposition.

However, with the fall of the Soviet Union, Washington made the decision to disband us, since the Kremlin had sent its undercover troops to the unemployment line. But that turned out to be a wrong move in the near future. Most of the Soviet agents who were displaced soon returned to the ring as part of a new affiliation, transformed into *boyeviks*, the well-trained enforcers who in the 1990s made up a feared "black army" for several clans of The Organization, a very powerful global crime syndicate also known as the *Organizatsiya*....

In other words: The Russian Mafia.

Hi, folks, my name is Patrick Coonan, but in the trade, I'm known as Agent Delta.

*C*hapter *1*

FELDMAN, OCF

Right in the heart of Washington, D.C., an impressive building of gargantuan dimensions was built at the end of the second half of the 1990s. Most of the citizens who live in the U.S. Capitol will never know what mysteries are hidden in the hallways and offices of this monstrous complex built out of heavy glass panels, stainless steel, and concrete. They can't even guess the meaning of the initials engraved — not painted in a striking color so as not to attract too much attention — that can be seen in the upper left corner of the structure's pavilion. Only three characters, three letters as anonymous as they are lonesome: O, C, F.

On a warm June summer night, a tall man, sort of thin but with an incipient pot belly, baring Lincolnesque features that gave him a somewhat patriarchal look, walked through the desolate hallway of the East Wing of said building. He had thick silver hair that his high-class stylist kept impeccably trimmed (at two hundred and fifty dollars a cut, taxpayers' money). His reddish skin gave him a fresh appearance and his thick black eyebrows were the focal point on his entire long face.

This individual did not carry a briefcase, but in that building, the OCF's Washington headquarters, no one had use for them since no information printed on paper was ever allowed to leave the premises. Any official agency data he uploaded, if he did, was encrypted on the hard drive of a tiny electronic board that at the time was considered "the latest high-tech innovation." Nowadays, of course, they are as common as the name John Smith and have been brought to the market under rather peculiar brand labels, such as BlackBerry, Sidekick LX, LG, and iPhone. The tall gray-haired man was carrying one of those curious gadgets.

This certainly said a lot about the individual. He was no fool, of course. Not even an obscure executive of that colossal and semi-anonymous new security agency of the federal government. He was the *head* of the entire organization.

The thick concrete gate that isolated his office from the corridor only showed, also engraved in the asphalt, the initials G.D. and everyone who had access to the innards of the modern construction knew well what they stood for: "General Director."

The G.D. entered his workplace; the office seemed to have the same dimensions as any golf course. It even had a space conditioned to serve as a gym for the occupant with a jogging mat, a stationary bicycle, and a Universal weight-lifting machine. It also contained one of those metal and Plexiglass capsules attached to ultraviolet light bulbs that the rich and famous often employ to tan their skin.

The door closed automatically behind the G.D. and since it was a "smart building" with just a few oral commands the tall gray-haired gent managed to turn on the lights in the office and dim them; the Black & Decker percolator was also activated and started brewing coffee, and the latest generation computer resting on the large desk came to life. Before Director Feldman parked his slender buttocks on the padded seat of the high-backed swivel chair, the intercom on his desk buzzed and the voice of his secretary was heard:

"Good evening, sir."

Feldman scratched his nose and replied: "Hi, Sally. What's up?" while walking towards the coffee strainer.

"I just sent the data I received from the Moscow Bureau to your terminal, sir. Oh, and I also wanted to inform you that this afternoon I sent Agent Long's transfer request to Superintendent Jenkins; it was approved, sir."

His secretary's comment amused him. "Of course, it was approved," he muttered to himself, "Jenkins had no alternative."

"Mortimer Long will arrive in Washington, D.C. tomorrow morning, sir."

Feldman stopped and frowned. "That needs to be changed," he said, "let Mr. Jenkins know that this is not where I'm going to need Long; have him fly directly to Miami, I will meet him at the Biltmore Hotel in Coral Gables."

"Very good, sir. Anything else?"

"Yes. Get my personal jet ready to take off in a couple of hours; I must get to Miami tonight."

"Will do, sir."

Without wasting time, Feldman finished making himself a coffee, to which he added cream, but no sugar. He occupied his imperial desk and dedicated himself to reviewing all the material drawn from the shared files of the legendary Moscow Bureau. Well, that "legendary" adjective was only employed among themselves, of course, we at the Quadrille — being a considerably much smaller outfit— managed to inflict considerably more damage in the battle against the Russian Mafia clans than the entire OCF with all its divisions around the globe....

But let's not go into that now and get on with the story.

The first thing Arnold Feldman noticed on his computer screen was old Yuri Pavenko's file; I suppose his record must have impressed him. Yuri had been a very dangerous adversary during the Cold War, when he was in his prime; as a matter of fact, he still was, but Feldman was not aware of it until that warm June night when fate, as capricious as ever, caused the now-turned Russian weapons dealer to cross his path.

"Holy cow!" He spat and, frowning, leaned over the screen to devote himself fully to reading the data coming in with rising interest.

Truth be told, the Russian's story could impress anybody.

His grandfather had been a career military man, an honorary graduate of the notorious Frunze Academy and a decorated hero of World War II. Pavenko's dad did not follow in the grandfather's footsteps because he had a bohemian spirit, but little Yuri did inherit the Pavenkos' inclination to wage war, only he did not pursue a career in the army as was customary in that family. After completing the obligatory youth period of military service, he left the Red Army troops to join the ranks of the mighty KGB. A more in-depth study of the reason that motivated him to break the mold would probably show that it had to do with his tendency toward obesity; being overweight while in the military is not practical. But Yuri more than proved during the Cold War that obesity was never an impediment for him, and a hundred battalions of regular soldiers from the Warsaw Pact were never more dangerous to NATO than one single Yuri Pavenko, that chubby operative with a mixed character (sometimes malicious, sometimes good-natured) whose peculiar voice was as hoarse and harsh as that of a troglodyte.

When Prime Minister Andropov ordered the KGB to neutralize the threat that Ronald Reagan's *Pershing II* missiles posed to the Kremlin's designs, the KGB commanders in the Soviet Union decided to activate a plan cooked up and carried out by their Atomic Fang Division to blow Manhattan off the face of the Earth. Yuri Pavenko was the sleeper agent that Directorate S chose to lead the operation in New York, the only one as far as I knew who was still alive despite the 9mm slugs I'd poked him with during a fierce gun battle in the port of Manhattan.

Of course, I would not learn about this until Mr. Feldman, and his goddamned Moscow Bureau, stuck their noses in the matter.

*C*hapter 2

GOODBYE, HAPPY DAYS!

Miami Beach, Florida.

It was the summer of 2000 and the hotel where I was staying, the Newport Beach Crowne Plaza Resort, was the ideal place for an exhausted government agent to spend his well-deserved R & R. In fact, that's exactly what I was doing at that moment. My boss had agreed to grant me a few days' leave, but not before sternly warning me to remain ready for action in case of an emergency; you know the drill. That's why I didn't flinch when the messenger arrived; as they say, I'd been warned. However, the contact he used on that occasion broke the mold to which he had accustomed me.

Col. Marlon Berkowitz was a clever man, and he knew very well how to handle things. Dealing with senior agents, who do not always accept his inopportune calls willingly, had made him develop very creative methods for summoning us back into action; especially to hook the oldest and most rebellious of our outfit. Not that I consider myself exactly an old man, but at forty, most of my colleagues at CI5 seem like kids.

A couple of years had already gone by since Red Goliath's death and the inexorable expansionism of the

Russian Mafia's operations on the American continent gave food for thought to certain Washington bureaucrats who finally decided to get the Quadrille out of the limbo in which the cessation had plunged it. The Cold War might be over, yes, and many of the operatives who'd originally closed our ranks were no longer in position to return and with a few reservations — among which I include myself, of course. Of those "dinosaurs" suitable for clandestine warfare there were only two specimens left: The other one was a former CIA man named Alfred Tilson, my original Quadrille instructor. It was then that the Colonel was forced to recruit again and accept that he and his affected troops needed to become part of a much larger and complex agency, the Organized Crime Force, which by the end of the 1990s counted with several divisions spread over North, South and Central America, Western and Eastern Europe. Almost no one ever called her by her real name, Arnold Feldman's mother-organization was better known by its 3-letter acronym: OCF.

The new agents that my boss hired to reform his troops were mostly New Age kids, skillful in the use of computers and electronic tablets, expert hackers who constantly searched for information in that un-fathomable labyrinth — well, unfathomable to me, that is — consisting of binary codes and cyber networks. They all looked pretty good, and believe me, standing in front of a cardboard target, these new kids were lions capable of grouping more shots on the bullseye than old William Tell himself in the days of bows and arrows. But when it came time to kill with an edged weapon from behind, in cold blood, they hesitated like school children, no matter how many degrees they held in karate, aikido or Tae kwon do. That is what the new Quadrille had transmuted into then, once it became a subsection of the OCF. The old moniker under which we operated vanished as if by magic and they began to call us CI5 (Counterintelligence 5) within the infrastructure of this new almighty mother agency.

Anyway, the agent that my boss chose to serve as messenger that day was none other than my current partner, also part of that new breed of smart operatives. We all had to work with partners these days, because the general director of the OCF, Mr. Arnold *fuckin'* Feldman, had made it a rule. I suppose that he sought to make it clear that the era of the "lone wolves" was past and behind us. Of course, Agent Phi — that was her code name — was not exactly an easy partner to get along with; she had a rebellious and extremely combative spirit and never let herself be easily defeated by any Russian thug, much less daunted by the mockery or contempt of her male colleagues. I always remember her as someone who walked with her head held high and a chip on her shoulder. Despite my old precepts, I must admit I liked her a lot from the beginning — perhaps I was influenced by the dynamics of her youth, her magnetic beauty, and that carnal sensuality that you breathed in her. She had a *very* high degree of sex appeal, something I always found useful in the line of duty. I disposed of many enemies attacking from the rear while they stood in awe admiring her curves....

Well, something like that.

When I discovered Jessica approaching the Jacuzzi where I was enjoying myself on the little paved path that bordered the Olympic pool, I prepared for the worst. My instinct told me that, despite being dressed in a bathing suit (a minuscule thong that left very little to the imagination), her presence at the Newport Beach Hotel was not exactly due to recreational purposes. That's what I would have wished, what the hell... I'd always dreamed of taking her to bed since I laid eyes on her for the first time.

Before reaching my side, Phi stopped by an outdoor bar and ordered a *Piña Colada*. While she waited to be served, I had the opportunity to contemplate her at my ease. Of medium height and with lush red hair, very fine and pale skin that did not tan well under the sun. Hers was a solid and curvy body, in the prime of her twenty-six years, that, sometimes, when we started running, made me painfully aware of my age (my exaggerated taste for red meat and beer had introduced gout and arthritis to my life). Although her legs were well defined by the traces of athletic muscles, the fact did not detract from the femininity of her figure. Her breasts — sometimes I can't talk about them without losing composure — were certainly generous, like two ovals of smooth flesh that were squeezed inside the bra where they were now swaying on that sunny summer morning. Of course, those who know the South Beach area would not have found Jessica as outrageously exhibitionist as she seemed to me at that moment. In South Beach she would have been taken for a moderate girl because there are few women there who cover their breasts in public, but that area is infested with liberated local femmes and Canadian tourists. Although it sometimes attracts professional snoops, like yours truly.

In contrast, the hotel where I was staying was located at the northern end of Miami Beach, an area known as Sunny Isles, where billionaire investors like Donald Trump have built luxury condo towers in the hope of turning this zone into an American twin sister of the French Riviera. Here Phi was an eye-catcher, though of all those who stared at her — the men in pleasant fascination and most women with envy — very few would have suspected that they were in the presence of a trained agent, capable of killing in cold blood.

I studied her carefully the entire time she took to approach me. The blood began to fizz in my veins and certainly not because of the hydraulic massage my body was receiving in the Jacuzzi. I was wearing a pair of sunglasses whose dark lenses prevented Phi from knowing where I was looking, but I was sure she had already spotted me among the vacationers. She scanned the area with her eyes and then stood straight before me, blocking the sun from my view with her adorable figure.

"Miss Fitts! What a pleasant surprise!" I exclaimed, calling her by her last name. Anyone who had been watching us would have thought she was my secretary, or an assistant of sorts. At that time, it wasn't far from the truth. Jessica Fitts functioned as a field agent, as well as an analyst, something that would change over time. "I didn't know you were on vacation...."

"Good morning, Mr. Prince," she addressed me in a teasing low voice, "would Your Majesty mind sharing the Jacuzzi with me?"

Her playful smile didn't reveal much, but that didn't mean anything; in our profession, cynicism is just another tool.

"Certainly not, Your Highness, you are always welcome. Jump in." With these words I returned her playful grin — and the cynicism too. I couldn't help but follow with my eyes the sway of her breasts as she entered the effervescent waters of the small pond. My criterion in such cases, I always stick to it, is to stare at whoever cares to show me such a lovely pair of "knockers."

I grabbed the glass that was resting on the tiles near my right hand and took a swig of whiskey.

"You look terribly good for a man of your age, Pat," she said, "your muscle tone is still tense, and you have acquired an enviable tan that brightens the blue of your eyes... What have you done, Mr. Dorian Gray, make a pact with the devil? You look good enough to eat," she sighed.

I glanced at my wristwatch, pretending to be in-different to the crude compliment she gave me, if that was what it was, but even though I knew it was a joke between comrades, I was pleased to imagine that she was sincere. Age makes us more sensitive; don't you know?

"I hope so, precious; I've been sunbathing for several days now and, if my calculations are correct, I still have a couple more weeks left without doing much."

"Ha! Don't even think about it."

I grinned. "Well, that figures. After seeing you arrive, I thought my vacation was shot to hell."

"You're not wrong; the Old Man wants you back."

"The Old Man, you say... He wants me back. So, it is confirmed then, goodbye to happy days!"

Normally, the term "wanted back" for a CI5 agent means drop whatever it is you're doing and immediately show up at our offices in Midtown Miami, a massive Art Nouveau building located in the business district. But the curious thing about the situation (and this is why I think the Colonel picked Miss Fitts to cut short my time off) was that at that moment I did not feel as frustrated as I usually do in such circumstances. It was clear that having the charming Agent Phi here with me, half naked in front of my very eyes, was some kind of "analgesic."

"Hell, this isn't fair," I protested with some reluctance.

"Come on, dearie, you've been resting for more than a week..., besides," and when she paused, I thought I noticed a certain seductive nuance in her soft voice, but she could also be playing with me because we always flirted without getting to anything serious, "we don't have to show ourselves immediately at headquarters."

"Oh, really? And how do you explain that?"

"The Old Man's instructions were to contact you at the hotel and then take a plane flight, tomorrow afternoon, to Cali, Colombia. He will be waiting for us down there."

"Cali... He said Santiago de Cali, are you sure? He could have meant California."

"I'm sure, Pat!" she snapped in a suddenly biting tone, the opposite of the sexy, persuasive pitch she had employed only seconds before. The same tone she always uses when I question her words. "Cali, I said," she confirmed.

I remained silent for a few seconds, trying to digest the news; it certainly was a drastic change. I reached for a pack of cigarettes and the disposable lighter that was resting next to my drink and lit one.

"Can you offer me one?" Jessica asked.

"I didn't know you smoked," I replied, "I warn you; I don't like women who taste or smell like an ashtray."

She grinned and extended her hand to accept the ciggie I lit for her. "I don't do it often, you know, but sometimes, when I consume alcohol, it motivates me to take one to my lips."

As she spoke, I noticed the beads of sweat that the bright Florida sun had placed on her upper lip and the bridge of her nose.

"What a waste, Carrots. Is that the only thing you like to put in your mouth when you drink?

She took it well. Nowadays you must be careful with the female colleagues. Any joke with erotic overtones can end up in a complaint for sexual harassment between co-workers, and even more so now that we were no longer employed by a clandestine outfit but were part of the large family of federal agencies.

"What?!" she exclaimed, then started laughing.

"I assure you that there are many things that taste better than sucking on a cigarette. I mean if you insist on taking 'something' to your lips, right?

What are you doing, you moron? I thought, furious with myself for that slip. But with my attractive female companion, so close and half naked before my very eyes, it was quite difficult for any red-blooded heterosexual male to maintain control of the hormonal impulses.

Jessica threw a sharp glance at me and sighed. "You know, I better let that pass," she said, becoming serious after a fashion. "If necessary," she added deliberately, "I can also tell *you* the same thing, can't I?"

I drew a long breath and responded with: "I wish you'd dare, Carrots. I suspect we've both been longing for this...."

My last words generated a tense silence. I have already said that we always flirted during our job interaction, but I know that in that moment everything suddenly changed, the flirtation moved from the sensual to the sexual; all traces of foreplay vanished and only Jessica and I were left there, with our bare feelings.

"Maybe *you* should think better about what you say before you open that big mouth of yours, Agent Coonan," she whispered very seriously. "It's preferable not to start any fires that we are not prepared to suffocate, don't you think?"

I confess that, despite the apparent gravity of the situation, I was amused by the severity with which she articulated those last words. I had to hold back a smile when I realized, once more, how fickle some women tend to be. This girl, just minutes before, had given me to understand that she was attracted to me ("you look good enough to eat," she'd said, remember?) and now she was putting on a spectacle for being the target of a similar comment.

I said: "No shit, Carrots, I'm more than ready to put out any fire that breaks out between us," I assured her. "Since you are the one bringing up the subject, I'm not going to deny it. It's as good a time as any to confess I have a crush on you, *chiquita*... but I warn you, I'm not going to propose to you just to get you in bed with me," I added teasingly afterwards to soften things up a bit, after all it had been a crude pass. "Let that be clear, eh."

"Seriously?" she said, and her sweet lips spread into a sly smile. "And who the hell is talking about marriage?"

Our first sexual encounter was not performed precisely in bed, it was consumed in the shower sometime later, when, already tired of splashing and fondling ourselves in the pool, we went up to the room. The curious thing, despite all that had been drilled into my psyche by the Quadrille instructors of long ago, was that I was able to abandon myself in the arms of Miss Fitts, as I'd never been able to do before with another female professional agent — allied or otherwise. Contrary to what Hollywood movies or TV shows might lead you to believe about the "glamorous lives" of spies and counterspies, in our chosen trade, quality sex doesn't come easily. One cannot afford to sleep with just about anyone, since we are always in the enemy's sight and there are certain security measures we must take. The Russians, for instance, have always been experts at fabricating sexual scandals and eliminating targets using the old tactic of the seductive assassin. But making love to Phi had its compensations, since she belonged to our pack.

In the shower stall, turning herself around to lean forward facing the bathroom wall, she asked me to soap her back. More than a pleading, it sounded like an order given in a hoarse growl that escaped from her throat, giving me a glimpse of a world of the young redhead's repressed desires. I took the bar of soap and began to slide it over her fine sweet-scented skin until she was completely soapy; then I began softly spreading the foam over her waist and hips with the palms of my hands. She arched her back, sighed with delight, and pushed her fleshy bums toward me.

"Damn, Jessica," I said, my voice suddenly hoarse, "have I ever mentioned you what an incredible ass you have?"

As I leaned forward to whisper in her ear, I rubbed against her.

"You just did, *querido*. Why tell me now?" her voice trailed off teasingly.

I experienced an intense fire burning in my groin, followed by the explosive hardening of my body. This must have been the reaction she was expecting because, resting her forehead on a bent arm against the wall, she thrust her formidable derriere in my direction.

I will only say that the pleasure Jessica gave me on that lazy summer afternoon is one of my most cherished memories....

Chapter 3

WONDER BOY LONG

Following the Colonel's instructions to the letter, we landed at Palmaseca Airport, in Santiago de Cali, the next night. The first phase of the journey was completed aboard a 727 jet on a commercial flight of *Aerolíneas Avianca*. The plane flew directly from Miami to Bogota and there we were greeted by an OCF reception committee: two minor agents, one of whom helped us go through the standard Customs procedures with a speed more typical of red-carpet diplomats than a couple of gringo operatives from an obscure branch of the Organized Crime Force. Then we climbed aboard another jet, this one private and much more compact, which according to the logo proudly stamped on its fuselage belonged to the OCF. And this is how we arrived in Cali.

At the Palmaseca airfield we were picked up by two OCF big guns and a representative of the Colombian National Security Service. His name was César Zambrano Lora, my two countrymen turned out to be agents Jamie Billings and Mortimer Long.

"Howdy, partners," I greeted with a false smile, I did not like the attitude of my compatriots in the least; they acted as if they both belonged to some kind of elite task force and we were the trash piled up in a corner of the attic, "are you guys permanently stationed here?"

"I am, for the moment," Billings replied, "I move around a lot. This is my fifth week in Santiago de Cali. Agent Long, on the other hand, has just arrived from Miami, but he is also with the Moscow Bureau and is new to these parts," Billings grinned and his round, ruddy face, typical of the classic American hillbilly, lit up with jovial malice, "just like the two of you."

Long was not; I mean he barely reached five feet tall, five two at the most, and wore his light brown hair in a military crewcut. His face was a hard mass of angular features, which fit very well with the strength displayed by his muscle-bound anatomy. It was obvious that he spent lots of his time lifting weights and when he shook my hand, he tried to crush my knuckles, naturally, but I didn't let him. The incident gave rise to an acute feeling of mutual contempt between the two of us. Of course, I struggled to control myself and focus my mind on more relevant issues, so as not to succumb to the over-powering temptation of kicking his kneecaps off. In theory, we are all supposed to be a big brotherly family of Justice Department agents united by the adverse circumstances of our trade, but in practice it doesn't work exactly like that. The truth is that these guys from the Moscow Bureau — alias "The Moscow Club," as my boss called it — all suffered from a bitter superiority complex.

"Oh!" I heard Phi exclaim. "You are one of those, aren't you?"

Long didn't know how to take it, he wasn't sure, but since I know Jessica well, I realized right away that she was making fun of him. The slight tone of sarcasm in her voice was unmistakable. But our cocky colleague did not hesitate in the slightest, instead, he chose to expand his broad, over-muscled chest and declare:

"You bet I am! I've been operating out of Moscow for two and a half years now." His voice resounded with pride when he nudged Billings in the back with the back of his hand and asked him. "Right, Jamie?"

Billings grunted and nodded his head without taking his eyes off the road.

"Moscow Bureau, eh. A most interesting office, without a doubt," I commented in a concise tone that downplayed the importance of his statement as I turned to our hillbilly chauffeur, who suddenly seemed like the nicest of the two.

"And you, Agent Billings, can you tell us anything about this operation?"

The man flashed a weak smile and said: "All in good time, Agent Coonan, all in good time. The director and your section chief are both already waiting to brief you. My mission is to make sure that the three of you arrive safe and sound at the meeting, as quickly as possible."

I said, "I see." But the way he said it, especially emphasizing *the three of you* made me grin. He was going to need a lot of luck to be able to pull it off.

Despite the tension in the cabin of the car, we made the trip to the National Gendarmerie without any setbacks. Although during the time it lasted, I struggled with my conscience not to beat the crap out of Mortimer Long — truth is that I despise these narcissists with bloated chests. Once we reached our destination, Billings and Mr. Zambrano Lora guided us through a corridor that hummed with frantic activity. Both uniformed and plainclothes agents moved from one place to another carrying briefcases and files. Finally, we entered a large underground office, marked BLOQUE

DE BÚSQUEDA at the entrance with large capital letters, where there were several people already waiting for us. I recognized the Colombian general immediately; his face had been appearing quite frequently in recent times in important American newspapers and magazines such as *USA Today*, *The Washington Post*, *The Miami Herald*, *Times Magazine*, and *Newsweek*. It was General Bartolo Cedeño, the experienced leader of the Search Bloc. The second authoritarian individual in that office was also known to me, of course. He was nothing more and nothing less than the highest living authority in the entire OCF.

The third man was my chief.

Chapter 4

THE SCORPION

As we approached the conference table the three men stood up and followed with introductions and a crisp handshake. I'd never had the opportunity to see Arnold Feldman in the flesh, only in photos and videos, and the first impression I got of him was that of a very theatrical gent, with an air of arrogance so strong it stank. I know my boss well, and it was not difficult for me to notice the high degree of tension this meeting caused him, although at that moment I was not able to fully grasp why. I put this down to the fact that our subsection, CI5, was not exactly a popular branch within the parent agency, which posed a question: *What the hell were we doing here?*

"Very well," the Colonel spoke, addressing me, "since we are all gathered, Agents Coonan and Fitts, I will begin by emphasizing the importance and the extraordinary nature of this operation. Circumstances force us to work shoulder to shoulder with..." he paused to look up quickly and point his chin at Mortimer Long, "the Moscow Bureau, and, of course, the Colombian Search Bloc led by General Cedeño, who is eager to speak. But, since his English is quite limited, his aide-de-camp, Mr.

Zambrano Lora here, will serve as his official interpreter."

Zambrano looked at his superior and General Cedeño began to speak in Spanish, a language I was fluent in, but which I was not sure was the case with Wonder boy Long of the Moscow Bureau, and probably not with our General Director either. Both seemed to be the kind of gringos who never try to learn other people's languages and think that the rest of the world is obliged to speak English. Well, to each his own. General Cedeño went straight to the point, he expressed himself with short sentences and energetic gestures while he explained to us how worrying the current situation was for the Colombian government. A gent named Carlos Rafael Arteaga, nicknamed *El Alacrán* — that's Spanish for The Scorpion — had recently come to occupy the vacant throne of the Cali Cartel, or so I'd understood, after the capture and deportation to the USA of the Rodríguez Orejuela brothers and their partner, José Santacruz Londoño. When he finished, he gave the floor to his assistant, César.

"Before proceeding to review the information we have about Don Carlos, I want you to tell us a little about the Russian Mafia. I admit that we are not very well-versed in this issue here, which is why we have gone to the United States government asking for the assistance of the OCF. We truly need some guidance on this matter."

Zambrano stopped to look directly at the Colonel, as if expecting it would be my boss who'd take the floor to give the orientation that the Colombians wanted regarding the present activities of the *Organizatsiya* in the American continent. My partner, Jessica, and I exchanged a knowing look, but immediately realized that was a mistake when the Colonel tried to make amends by clearing his throat and saying:

"Thank you, Mr. Zambrano, but please explain to the general that Washington has appointed Director Feldman as the overall coordinator of this operation and, in addition to being my superior, he is the official liaison of the U.S. government with your country's authorities, *he* is the one in charge of briefing you."

With a casual smile he turned to Feldman and concluded: "Go ahead, sir; you have the floor."

"The Russian Mafia," Feldman began, ignoring the Colonel completely and keeping his eyes fixed on those of General Cedeño, as if no one else were present in the room, "is an extremely dangerous international ring, which is consolidating itself among all the criminal organizations around the world. They are rapidly becoming a worrying fact, not only to Washington, but for the rest of the Western World *and* for our Russian friends as well, as they themselves have expressed...."

I could not help but grimace in disgust when he said, "our Russian friends", this was something hard for me to swallow after having spent the best part of two decades shooting it out with those people, but I managed to restrain myself and conceal my disgust with a faked cough that didn't fool my boss at all — to tell the truth, I never meant to.

"The new authorities in Russia," continued Director Feldman, "are not capable of dealing by themselves with what their own leaders call the *Organizatsiya*, which is why the Organized Crime Force was authorized by both governments to set up and operate one of its many divisions in Moscow. I could, of course, expand on the subject, but I prefer that Agent Mortimer Long do so. He is one of our best experts stationed in Moscow."

In all honesty, the lad did an excellent job with the brilliant, in-depth, and detailed overview of Russian Mafia activities that he convinced us. I confess that I've never been an expert on the subject, but Jessica, who was more aware because she was always involved in the analytical phase of our operations, gave me a sharp sidelong glance which I interpreted as "this guy knows his stuff." Summarizing, Morty Long enlightened us on the formation of the nine most powerful clans that made up the *Organizatsiya* at that time, focusing mostly on the one led by the brothers Pavel and Oleg Ostrovsky, which would give so much trouble to CI5 and which, as it was proved later in history, was the one that caused the most damage in the entire American continent.

The Colonel let him talk as he pleased without interrupting him for a long while once he understood how fascinated the Colombians were with Long's enthralling overview, but I, who knew Marlon Berkowitz well, picked up immediately when he began to turn impatient. He was one of those men who does not take kindly to anyone calling the shots for long — anyone other than himself, that is. Call him a narcissist if you will. Finally, when he felt he could divert the general attention to the specific issue that had brought us all to Cali, without disrespecting Director Feldman and his prima donna from the Moscow Bureau, of course, he cleared his throat loudly and took the floor:

"Thank you for your *brilliant* dissertation, Mr. Long, it's nice to work with agents like you," he added to be politically correct, "but returning to the Cali Cartel and its new frontrunner, Mr. Zambrano, you mentioned something related to a new caste of drug dealers, which the Search Bloc has tagged as *traquetos*. I assume that Carlos Rafael Arteaga belongs to the kind, correct?"

Long looked at Feldman in disbelief, surprised by the interruption. Feldman opened his mouth as if to protest my boss's uncalled for interference, but after thinking it over he signaled to the Moscow Bureau man to stand down and let the ball roll by.

"That is correct, Colonel," Zambrano said with the consent of his superior. "But let's be clear on one thing: the Cali Cartel, as we knew it, disbanded with the extradition of its three leaders to your country. For them there is no going back. What is happening now in Colombia is a mutation of the gangs, you could say, and this one we are now facing is the *Norte del Valle Cartel*, they are taking steps to take over the place. *El Alacrán* is one of the leaders, yes: perhaps the most dangerous. He is bold and unscrupulous; many fear him. We are going back to the times of Pablo Escobar and his ill-fated Medellin Cartel because this type of element has stolen the peace and joy that was once experienced on the streets of Cali. Crime has increased drastically these days, gentlemen. And that's not counting Marulanda's guerrillas, who are also giving us a lot of problems. Watch the screen, *caballeros*, that is him...."

There we finally had *El Alacrán*, The Scorpion. His was a hard face to forget, with typical indigenous features: cooper-brown skin, flattened features, oblique eyes, a wide and bulging nose, and very thick African lips. He had a bull's neck and wore his frizzy hair dyed in ochre color locks, Valderrama-style, a fashion then favored by lots of Colombian young men.

"An ugly duckling," commented Morty Long, for whom anyone who wasn't white, blond, and blue-eyed was probably ugly.

"And very cunning too, Mr. Long. Very cunning and dangerous; don't underestimate the man by his looks," added General Cedeño in his broken English while frowning.

"We knew he was a very tough nut to crack," went on Zambrano, "even before we found out the kind of company he keeps these days. Now, you'll see..."

A pause and then, abruptly, the image on the screen evolved and the room seemed to start spinning around me. The new face that had just materialized looked dangerously familiar... Oh, yes! It was the kind of face my chief and I could relate to from a bygone era. And then I realized the true purpose of our presence in Santiago de Cali. And when I say "our" I mean specifically the former operatives of Col. Berkowitz's Quadrille, not this new subsection named CI5 that operated in the shadow of the OCF. Well, perhaps the Moscow Bureau could also feel directly related to that face; many things had changed in the New World Order, but the mug shot that now loomed on the screen belonged to a ghost from the past.

Chapter 5

DEAD DEMONS

My boss asked: "Do you recognize him, Agent Coonan?"

If we had been sitting at our Midtown office building in Miami, he would never have called me "Agent Coonan". For him I was always Delta around headquarters.

"Yes, sir; I do. A demon from the grave."

"And you, Director Feldman?" inquired the Colonel, addressing the fop Washington had chosen to rule us in the new millennium.

"Jesus, what a question!" Feldman grumbled in annoyance.

Marlon Berkowitz suppressed a cynical smile; his interjection had been a tricky one.

"Given the current circumstances surrounding the reappearance of this character," spoke the Colonel with calculated phlegm, "I only intend to establish that all of us are aware of who he is; that's all. This is the image captured by the agents of the Search Bloc in a nightclub in Juanchito, not the one kept in our files. Anyway, we all agree it's him then, don't we?"

And he looked at all of us deliberately, one by one, with his intense laser beam gaze that had the power to penetrate your skull all the way through the encephalon.

"It *is* Yuri Pavenko," retorted Morty Long in a hoarse voice, "alive and kicking. Older, yes, and perhaps a bit thinner, but it's him."

"No doubt about it!" snapped Feldman.

"All right," said the Colonel, "having clarified the point and because everyone here agrees as to who this man is, I'll ask Agent Long to share his information with us. I've been hearing rumors that our Moscow colleagues are tracking him down...."

Long looked at Feldman and Feldman at my boss, chewing him up with malevolent eyes, but Marlon Berkowitz adopted a funny saintly expression. I almost laughed in their faces. Of course, as I mentioned earlier, Pavenko and the Quadrille had history, a history as long and ugly as an overgrown snake out of the Amazonian jungle, the outcome of which could have triggered a nuclear war*.

Director Feldman swallowed his ire, at least for the moment, and silently gave the go-ahead to his Moscow Bureau boy, who began to speak.

"His full name is Yuri Ivanovich Pavenko and he was originally a member of the Soviet KGB..." he failed to mention that the Russian had been, perhaps, the best saboteur in their entire Atomic Fang Division, but very few people knew that, of course, "... and everything seems to indicate that, at present, he is an important member of the Ostrovsky clan, who operates out of Helsinki. The problem is that, nowadays, these Russian mobsters are going global. The Ostrovsky brothers are involved in just about *everything* ranging from bank fraud, extortion and narcotics smuggling to white slavery and organized exotic car theft...."

As Long continued with his didactic speech, the screen evolved and the photo of Yuri's mug was replaced by an image where he appeared full-length, seated at a table that he now shared with The Scorpion and another individual I was unable to identify. Pavenko seemed to have lost some weight, yes, but not a lot. I noticed that Phi was also interested in the third man.

"Excuse me, gentlemen," spoke out Jessica for the first time, "who is that mysterious man who conforms the trio?"

César Zambrano Lora answered: "It's very likely that he is a guerrilla commander."

"Mm... A Colombian guerrilla commander?" asked the Colonel, taking Long and the OCF's general director completely by surprise. "I'd say he looks more like a Muslim, or someone from the Middle East."

His unwavering words had a devastating effect. For a moment we all fell silent.

"Come on, gentlemen," Marlon Berkowitz continued after a short pause, "it's obvious to me that what's at stake here has nothing to do with drug trafficking."

"No? Why so sure, Colonel?" queried the Search Bloc leader.

"Well, Agent Long and his colleagues from the Moscow Bureau probably know this," he pointed out gravely, "but the Yuri Pavenko that we once knew only specialized in *one* thing, General."

"Smuggling state-of-the-art military equipment," intervened Long.

"And the so-called WMD," wrapped up my boss rather dramatically, "the Weapons of Mass Destruction."

"Exactly!" pontificated Feldman for the sake of exercising the last word, while Phi and I made a point to keep out of the fray between those three.

Of course, our mutual restraint was not going to last for long. This tense situation between Mr. Feldman, the Moscow Bureau maverick and us would soon come to a crisis.

*Refer to the first book in the series, entitled *The Quadrille* (Author's Note)

Chapter 6

STRATEGY & PLANS

Much later, in another very different room that belonged to a pleasant hotel named Las Mercedes, located in another sector of the Cali metropolis, the Colonel, Jessica and I held our own private conference. The suite was on the third floor and was quite spacious, with a double bed and a few other amenities. We were sitting on the balcony around a small round table and from that high vantage point, the hotel pool could be seen; there were still a few night swimmers kicking the water down there. It was almost 10 p.m. and a prevailing stillness hung over us like a smokescreen behind which sudden violence lurked.

"I know this operation is going to be difficult to carry out with the interference of the Moscow Bureau, especially that kid Long; he is too smart for his own good," the Colonel said with a sour smile. "I've heard that he's a crazy horse, but also that he's a competent operative. Probably the best Mr. Feldman has in all Eastern Europe."

I looked at my boss and grimaced, the same way I do when refraining from making biting remarks. I just lit a ciggie, taking advantage of the fact that we were on the balcony and the air flowing at that level prevented me from stinking up the room with the smell of tobacco.

"I have a bad feeling about the whole setup, Colonel, this mission will turn out to be a disaster," said Phi and I was glad she was the one to say it. Someone had to dare, right?

"Well...."

"Don't do it, Colonel," I said, backing her up, "you know it's not going to work. This operation stinks worse than a rotten fish. How the hell is this arrangement with the Moscow Club supposed to work, sir? We are not cops! Feldman's men operate completely differently than the way you taught us. They arrest and put criminals away, while we *don't*... At least we never did in the past!"

"Delta is right, sir," Jessica hissed in a passively severe tone.

"I know *that*, for God's sake!" my chief snapped. "Or do you think I'm blind? This situation is very irritable, yes, for me as well. It's like a thorn in my side that I can't pull out. But there have been a lot of changes on Capitol Hill and Washington preferred to annex us to the Justice Department, even though I continue to fight behind closed doors to regain our old status with the DOD and detach ourselves from the Organized Crime Force and this snobbish bastard," I presume he meant Feldman, "but let's not get ahead of ourselves, eh; we're obliged to work as part of the OCF for the time being. And I trust you both to accept that!"

He paused to watch us carefully. After a few seconds of tense silence, which both Phi and I respected, Marlon Berkowitz showed us a baleful grin that made the bristles on the back of my neck stand up. He was a man to be feared most when he smiled; I know that for a fact.

"However," he spoke again, "this does not mean that we must abide by all the whims of the Director. Right?"

"Phew! That's good to hear, sir," I breathed, "does

it mean we are going to take down Comrade Pavenko for good, instead of cooperating with his arrest. Or, God forbid, we have only come as observers and to advise?"

"That I have not yet decided, Delta," he answered with a frown, "I am tentatively inclined to eliminate him. Any way you look at it that man, alive, is a danger to humanity."

"Yuri Pavenko should have been removed long ago," sneaked in Jessica. "It's a miracle he escaped alive from his first encounter with Pat in the docks of Manhattan, during Operation Red Mushroom*... Well, don't look so startled, sir, I've been going through the old files we have on that man."

The Colonel drew a long breath. "That's right," he said, "at that time, I gave orders to take him out. It is not my fault that the operative tasked with the assignment couldn't fulfill this simple task."

He avoided looking my way when he said it, but he didn't have to. His poisoned dart had nailed the mark. But he was right, of course, the slip had been on me.

"I did my best to pull it off, Colonel," I heard myself mumble in a soggy voice.

"Well, it was your first mission with the Quadrille, and we all muddle up sooner or later. The past can't be undone, can it? Now we'll get a chance to make amends."

"Sure." I spoke. "I like that idea, sir... For a moment I thought you were going to order us to play cops and bandits with the opposition here, in Santiago de Cali."

I realized I'd gotten ahead of myself as soon as I saw him grin.

"In fact, that's what the two of you are going to do — officially, of course," he said, expanding his enigmatic grin. "A verdict has been passed in Washington that Pavenko must be stopped at all costs and thus prevent him from turning the southern end of our continent into a bazaar of Weapons of Mass Destruction... No one specified how and we only know one way of stopping scum of this kind: permanently. But that is not to be shared with our Moscow Bureau champ," he added, then winked, "it is a fact that some arrests get thwarted and the officers in charge of executing them end up shooting to kill in self-defense... I'm sure you are all familiar with the Mexican *ley de fuga*, right?"

Put in those terms, things sounded easy.

Easy... yeah... Just like that first assignment back in Manhattan, during Operation Red Mushroom, when I'd been given the order to take the bloody Russian down. But in all honesty, I never suspected that this present incident would conclude in the twisted way it ended, or who knows, maybe I did. What's certain is that Operation Scorpion Tail — as it was tagged in CI5's Shared Files — turned out to be a genuine Pandora's Box.

*Refer to the first book in the series, entitled *The Quadrille* (Author's Note).

Chapter 7

THE SCAPEGOATS

I should have suspected that nothing would change, I mean about our modus operandi and, specifically, the orders to eliminate Pavenko. The fact that I was in Colombia partly confirmed it, of course; we are only sent out of the country to pass the bill when both diplomacy fails, or when American justice oversteps its borders, but that had only happened on rare occasions. In my experience with the Quadrille, it had been only once. Thus, I was shocked at first to think that I was being sent to eliminate someone in a friendly foreign country like Colombia — that is why I'd questioned Jessica's information that glorious afternoon in North Miami Beach, when contacted by my redhead partner at the Newport Beach hotel. My only assignment outside the homeland, until now, had taken place in Moscow in the mid-1980s and it had been more than justified. My target: a high-ranking KGB officer; an assignment that had to be performed without sparking World War III*. Well, something like that.

But, as I've already said on previous occasions, the post-Cold War order had rapidly evolved, and our country was preparing itself for a new war. What I did not like, not in the least, was that we would have to do the fighting down here in South America, in the neighboring Mexico... or in any other Latin country in the southern hemisphere where the big drug cartels ruled. You know why? Because I had a feeling that, sooner or later, we would end up stepping on each other's toes. Many of Uncle Sam's big agencies would be competing to get the upper hand and competing among ourselves is a typical aspect of American sportsmanship. Sometimes we even go at it too hard for our own good.

"Okay," said my boss and cleared his throat out loud, "let's go over our operational plan then. The mission has been labeled Operation Scorpion Tail, for obvious reasons; however, the main target here is not The Scorpion, *comprende,* I repeat, your main target is not The Scorpion, but its tail."

"An *atomic* tail, sir?" murmured Phi.

"Exactly! We must be clear on this, you copy?" he insisted, staring grimly at me with those fiercely cold blue orbs of his, like the eyes of an Arctic wolf or an Eskimo dog. "With Pavenko in the picture, we must assume that there is a nuclear angle to all this, somewhere, perhaps even a biochemical one as well."

I conceded: "Yes, sir. Like you said: Weapons of Mass Destruction."

And he was right about that, of course. Yuri Pavenko had been trained in his youth as a nuclear saboteur. We could not turn our backs on that fact, even less ignore the danger that was coming. In Colombia itself there was a precedent for what the most powerful drug lords could do. A now-dead member of the defunct Medellin Cartel, the one known as Mexican Gacha, had hired the services of Israeli mercenaries to train his *sicarios* in the use of explosives and military weapons, including bazookas, grenade-launchers, and even mortars. We learned of this from the voice recordings taken by CIA spy planes where *El mexicano Gacha* expressed his desire to acquire a ballistic missile to fire it against the *Casa Nariño* (the Colombian equivalent to our White House) if those "motherfuckin' politicians" persisted in approving the extradition treaty to the United States.

"The Scorpion is also on the agenda," carried on my boss, "but only as a secondary target. You will take him down, if possible, as a favor to the Search Bloc. A favor that has not been officially requested, for the record, but one which General Cedeño has given me to understand would be well looked upon. How and when to do this is entirely up to you."

Having said this, the Colonel settled down behind the laptop he had brought with him and punched a few keys. "To allow *El Alacrán* and his organization to even think of acquiring WMD to do business with Muslim radicals would be... Let me see how I can put this... sheer insanity."

He paused to draw a long breath.

"The time has come to teach all these criminals a hard lesson, but we will do it our way, discreetly, and in a such a fashion that will resonate as a subtle, but categorical, message to the caverns of the Ostrovsky Clan; we will take down Pavenko and incidentally his newly found Colombian business partner, Don Carlos Arteaga."

"Any suggestions on how to go about the matter, sir?" inquired Jessica, frowning slightly.

"My strategy is simple, Phi, find a way to assemble

them and take them out at once. Expect interference from Agent Long, but I trust you two will find a way to deal with him," he paused briefly to wink at us, before adding. "Delta will take care of the tactics, as usual. For the time being I order you to remain quartered in Las Mercedes; I have people keeping the mark under surveillance. In the meantime, pretend to be a couple of gringo tourists on vacation in Colombia. I will ring you up when the time to act arrives."

"Yes, sir."

"Good. Between these four walls you have everything you need for now: maps of the city, two mobile phones and a satellite phone, and I'll leave you this computer. In due course I'll also get you the proper weapons. Don't forget that we are stepping on foreign soil."

With some concern, I began to notice how much he'd changed over the past few months; he was becoming more and more controlling with the passing of time; he was now also choosing the weapons we were supposed to employ to do the job, but I put it down to the fact that Mr. Feldman was keeping all of us under the loop and, unsurprisingly, the Colonel was worried that any out-side moves beyond his control would derail his career. And ours too.

"No, sir, we won't." I assured him and put a new ciggie to my lips. "Question, sir: we might want to go out and check out the city in the meantime. We'll need transportation."

"I see. Well, that can be arranged, Billings will serve as your chauffeur, or if you prefer, I can talk to César, General Cedeño's aide-de-camp. I will leave it to your choice."

His comment (*I will leave it to your choice*) made me scowl, he knew me well, this Marlon Berkowitz of the thousand devils, and probably had noticed in my countenance some sign of rebellion to his now almost constant manipulations.

"I didn't ask for a guide... sir," I clarified staring at him dourly, "just for permission to rent a car. Do we have that option, sir?"

Col. Berkowitz grinned with acid impatience. "Perhaps," he said softly, "but only if you deem it necessary. As thorny as our relationship with Director Feldman is, I don't want to be worrying about you two running amok in a foreign city."

"But it's obvious that Mr. Feldman needs us to catch Pavenko," said Jessica, "otherwise we wouldn't be here."

The Old Man looked at her with some asperity, as if expecting more from her, before turning to me: "Do you believe that too, Delta?" he asked softly.

I did not answer, because I considered it wiser to keep my trap shut until I learned from his own lips the true cause of so many concerns.

At my muteness, the Colonel drew a long breath and spoke: "Arnold Feldman has finally come across the opportunity to degrade us by discovering the presence of a live Yuri Pavenko in Colombia, a ghost from the past who should have been dead and buried a long time ago; especially after that plane crash reported in '98, where he was supposed to lose his life. We sent *you* to Bogota to confirm it, remember, *you*, the same Quadrille agent who was tasked with his physical elimination during Operation Red Mushroom in '84 and *failed* to finish him off, it was *you*, Delta, who confirmed the identity of the partially charred corpse that was recovered from the wreckage of the crash in Bogota... Why, you honestly believe that Mr. Feldman got us into this out of respect for our proficiency and looking for support for his man Long? Ha!"

He suddenly went silent and neither Jessica nor I could articulate a single word. He was furious.

"Don't be naïve, for Christ's sake! He has brought us here like lambs to the altar!" My chief shouted out of pure vehemence. "If this operation fails... *we* will be the scapegoats!"

*Refer to the first book in the series, entitled *The Quadrille* (Author's Note).

*C*hapter *8*

ALL KINDS OF DOUBTS

The Colonel spent a few more minutes with us and then left. Having nothing more to talk about for the moment — it was obvious that Jessica was not as concerned about the Old Man's allusions as I was — she excused herself and went into the bathroom to begin the complicated process of washing her hair and applying rejuvenating creams to her fine white skin. You know women, right? Even the most accomplished professionals always set aside a moment of their day to devote to these feminine beautifying functions. Hence, I found myself alone in the balcony, contemplating the stars of the Colombian night, beset by an uncomfortable feeling of anguished emptiness that crept under my diaphragm. I lit another cigarette to help me reflect and watched, for a few moments, as the last of the nocturnal swimmers began to leave the pool below due to the late hour.

Things were looking very ugly, indeed... Especially for me.

It's true that leaving loose ends in a profession like ours tends to create problems for the future, I will not deny that, and my failure to finish off Pavenko at the docks of Manhattan so many years ago was the cause of the effect we were now facing, but what cracked me most inside was not exactly that, what I could not understand at that particular moment was my boss' bizarre attitude... Why had the Colonel lied so blatantly in front of Jessica? What the hell was that direct allusion he had made, accusing me of having confirmed "the death" of Yuri Pavenko in a "plane crash" in Bogota?

This was the *first* time I'd heard about it!!!

I rubbed my forehead to relieve the tension knot that had grown between my brows. I stared grimly at the laptop the Colonel had left for us and placed it in front of me. Using my personal password, I entered the network that stored CI5 Shared Files and searched with dismay for the records registered during 1998, since according to my boss' words that had been the year Pavenko's alleged plane crash had occurred, and when I typed in my password into the system, I found to my surprise that I was denied access to the file! I broke out in a cold sweat... *What the fuck!* I thought. *What the hell is going on?* Angrily throwing the cigarette away I crushed it. I tried again to enter the system futilely, three times and nothing. But on the fourth attempt the screen opened a small rectangular window with some information that gave me a small glimmer of hope. According to what the log had registered, the operator who'd uploaded the data to the file and encoded it was someone I knew well, someone I trusted. Someone other than Jessica and Col. Berkowitz.

I went into the room and made sure that my partner was still in the bathroom. I tried opening the door with great stealth, but I couldn't, it had been locked from the inside. All right, that meant Phi didn't want to be disturbed in her beautification ritual, which suited me just fine. My next step was to get my hands on the satellite phone. The code on file belonged to Alfred Tilson, my master-instructor, one of the two surviving operators from the old Quadrille — the man who'd turned us all into cold-blooded killing machines. The remaining survivor was Agent Landon whose real name was Leo Balmaseda*, but that one didn't count because he'd been out of action for quite some time now, and I'd never heard of him again. It was rumored that he was in poor health, or something.

I returned to the balcony and pulled back the glass sliding panel that isolated it from the room, but instead of sitting at the table this time I leaned against the metal railing, keeping my eyes peeled on the bathroom door in case Jessica decided to come my way before I was done. I punched in Tilson's phone number, the one I carried in my memory; a personal one he once gave me in case I needed his help outside the unit. He answered the call on the second ring, it seemed as if he'd been waiting for my call.

"Yes?" his voice sounded cool and pleasant, not that of a man getting ready for bed.

"It's Pat, how are you, old sport?"

"I knew it was you. Nobody else has this number."

"Not even Col. Berkowitz?" I teased him.

"Especially not *him*." He said, and I could sense him smiling at the other end of the line.

"Tell me something, were you expecting the call?"

"Not really... Is there a problem?"

"There is, and a very serious one, I don't trust anyone else...."

"What about your new partner?

"You said it, she's new; you and I have known each other for a bunch of years now."

"And the Colonel? You don't trust *him*?" Tilson asked deliberately.

"Well, he is the problem... Or should I say part of it. The *real* problem is Director Feldman, it seems that the

Old Man is desperate, and I don't know why I have the feeling that I will end up being the sacrificial goat on behalf of our entire subdivision. I've just been told that Yuri Pavenko has been spotted in Colombia...."

"I heard something of the sort. The old Russian bastard... A ghost from the past!"

"I know his resurrection is my fault, I'm being haunted by the result of my first mission with the Quadrille; I should have finished him off instead of leaving him for dead in the Port of Manhattan, but I was so happy when I recovered the last component of that "dirty bomb" that... Aw, hell, there's no valid excuse. I fumbled it!"

"Don't taunt yourself, Pat," his warm, friendly voice cut me off, "we *all* make mistakes. Why do you think I ended up as master-instructor in the Quadrille? A mistake at Moscow Station when I was active with the CIA! We both know that to err is human."

"Yeah, but screwing up in our trade is to gamble with your life," I hesitated and could perceive the intensity of the bitterness reflected in my voice.

"Get to the point, Pat, what do you need?"

"Information."

"On what?"

"I just found out that I've been denied access to the 1998 files... *And* I just found out, from the Colonel, that in that year there was a plane crash reported in Bogotá where Yuri Pavenko's body was found and that it was me, listen to this, that I was the operative sent to the crash site to confirm the dead man's identity!"

"And it wasn't like that?" He asked.

"Jesus, no! Why the hell do you think I'm calling you?"

"I don't know, lad, why are you calling me, I had no knowledge of that either."

"Al..." I said, feeling the cold grip of fear beginning to strangle me, "you're fucking with me, aren't you?"

"Of course not! Why would you think that?"

"Damn it, because according to the registry, it was *you* who uploaded that year's files to the network! Mrs. Aledo was not with us at the time, I just read it on the screen!"

An ominous silence engulfed the connection for a few seconds. If I had been feeling bewildered before, when the Colonel first dropped the bombshell on me, I was completely lost now. My vision blurred for a few moments, and I had to force myself to take a couple of deep breaths to settle down.

"Pat, are you there?"

"Yes, Al, I'm still here."

"Look, I tried to access the network system just now, but it's down, which is strange, you know... Can you access it from your end?"

I rushed over to the computer, and, to my surprise, I could see that what Tilson said was true. The CI5 archive network was temporarily inoperative due to technical maintenance on the system.

"What the hell, I can't get in!" I exclaimed in furious anguish.

"Calm down, Pat. Maybe it's just a coincidence and maybe it's not. In any case, coincidences don't happen often in our trade, so it's best to presume that *someone* has been alerted by your several attempts to access that information and has temporarily knocked out the system."

"That's right!" I hissed.

"And that someone must be Marlon Berkowitz," he replied.

"Do you understand my dilemma now?"

"Yes, but be patient, a war warned does not kill soldiers. Obviously, the Colonel is up to something he doesn't want to share. I know Director Feldman has him under the loop, and us too, and that he's most likely using the Pavenko incident to screw us over; if so...."

"But why hasn't the Colonel come clean with me, why does this Yuri resurrection puzzle come up right this minute..., and why, dammit, is he holding me responsible for an identity verification I was never ordered to perform?"

"Good question. Let's do this, give me a little time to find out what I can on my own and we'll talk again; phone me tomorrow at this same time. Does that suit you?

I drew a long breath.

I had no choice.

I said yes.

*Refer to the first book in the series, entitled *The Quadrille* (Author's Note).

*C*hapter *9*

URBAN SAFARI

The next day was spent, for the most part, splashing around in the pool. All that time I was forced to fake in front of Jessica a nonchalance that I was far from feeling and that I managed to conceal with the erotic games we sustained in the pool, until my female partner lost her cool and challenged me to go upstairs and smother her uterine fires in our room. I'm not going to complain about it, quite the contrary; the sex she gave me was top-notch and a wonderful escape from the problem that overwhelmed me. In my mind still prevailed the memories of our encounter in the shower the day before, when we made love for the very first time, something that contributed to exacerbate my hormones.

As we entered the room, Jessica took my face in her hands, planted her lips over mine and began to devour my mouth with hers. We kissed passionately for a while, driving me crazy with her tongue repeatedly, until she decided to move her lips to other more erogenous areas of my body.

Sometime later — feeling much more relaxed — I left the bed quietly so as not to wake her up, since after several orgasms Phi had finally fallen asleep. In the kitchen I poured a Scotch and grabbed my cigarettes before reaching for the laptop and going to sit by the table on the terrace. The sun was beginning to set when I managed to connect to the Internet, but with no pretensions of accessing the CI5 archives again because if what I'd started to suspect turned out to be true, I wasn't going to find the network running today either. Instead, I spent my time surfing the net looking for information about Santiago de Cali, a city I did not know at all. My boss had said that until it was time to act, we were to play the role of a couple of gringo tourists looking for fun. So be it.

I began by realizing that Cali is not the kind of small town that we average North Americans are used to finding south of the border. I hate admitting it, but your average gringo thinks that the rest of the continent looks like some Mexican small border towns, dusty and uncivilized. The article I read, signed by one Krzysztof Dydysnki, described Santiago de Cali as "*a young, thriving, bustling metropolis with a population of approximately one million three hundred and thirty thousand, located in the Valley of the Cauca River. Its climate is warm and pleasant, almost tropical. Cali is well-known in Colombia for its powerful sugar industry but also for its music...*" That's what the article said. The music to which the Polish journalist was referring is the so-called "*salsa dura.*" Well, that's what they call it down there, in Colombia, but it's nothing more than a mixture of old rhythms coming from Cuba, Puerto Rico, and other regions of the Antilles.

"Salsa," I murmured to myself, "Mm...."

My mind raced back to New York, where sixteen years ago the nightmare had begun for me. And I remembered a Latin disco in Manhattan where on a Christmas night, at the end of 1983, one of the Russian AFD saboteurs named Yuri Pavenko had been contacted and activated by a Cuban operative of the KGB...

68

Hell, I was beginning to see it all very clear now. My past with Pavenko, unraveling itself before my mind's eye, was coming back to me gradually.

The file that Tilson stole through his CIA contacts, when we were sent to settle the score with old Kirov for having endangered our national security, stated that: *"Yuri Pavenko is a hedonist who fits perfectly into the rotten atmosphere that is lived in the big cities of Capitalism. Comrade Pavenko goes out of his way for expensive call girls, Western fashion clothes, high-tech home appliances, nightlife in exotic cabarets and extravagant nightclubs, luxury hotels. He is an admirer of Latin culture, women, and music."*

I pondered this information for several minutes before dismissing the idea that was germinating in my mind, but the notion came back right at me with the force of a locomotive, even though the Colonel had made it clear that he didn't want us running amok in the city doing our own thing... Perhaps, if the circumstances had been different, I would have stuck to his predilections, but his bizarre attitude had set me on guard and damned if I was going to stand by idly while others prepared the bonfire to roast me like a pig on Christmas Eve — even if, among those "others," was my own boss.

In the meeting held at the National Gendarmerie building with the Colombians, Director Feldman and his wonder boy Long, from the Moscow Bureau, Col. Berkowitz had mentioned that the photos of Pavenko conferring with The Scorpion and the unknown individual they had tagged as a "possible Muslim guerrilla leader," had been taken in a place called Juanchito. The name didn't tell me anything, of course, and at first, I thought it was an establishment of sorts, but when I entered Juanchito in the Internet search engine it turned out to be a suburb of the city where the most popular Cali salsa discos were located. The information pointed to Calle 5 between Carreras 38 and 44 — a special area for *rumberos*.

"*Comrade Pavenko is an admirer of the Latin culture, its women, and its music*," his dossier said; therefore, it was not illogical to think that my idea was well-founded. The plan was based on going out to have fun that night and scout around the marked location in search of a dance hall or *bailadero* where to find friend Yuri. Hell, perhaps it was a long shot, and we would not catch him, but the alternative of staying put in Las Mercedes without taking the shot was not an enticing prospect — not even having Jessica with me to enjoy more awesome sex.

Enough is enough. Inside me, the spirit of the hunter began to prevail. I was born in Denver, Colorado and spent the greater part of my adolescence stalking deer and elk up in the Rocky Mountains. This, added to years of experience as an underground operator, has taught me that inertia does not pay; inertia is a negative factor in many respects if you are accustomed to motion. Those hunters who sit still in the thicket are condemned to wait. And that was precisely my dilemma: My patience was running out. I didn't want to wait any longer. I was going to stir the pot a bit and pray for the opposition to feel threatened and come after me.

"Salsa..." I muttered.

I wondered how Jessica would react if I asked her to go out to party that night?

The Tourist Information & Culture Bureau was circulating a bulletin warning those foreigners passing through the city, who liked to walk the streets of Cali after 10 p.m., to refrain from doing so. There were plenty of reasons for that, of course, including an alarming pile of missing people and anonymous corpses; these were trying times of kidnappings and fierce guerrilla attacks, and local law enforcement could not guarantee everyone's safety.

Once I made up my mind, the next step to ponder was whether to communicate my intentions to my chief or go at it behind his back, but after careful consideration I opted for the former. I picked up one of the cell phones and punched in the contact number he had left us.

"Berkowitz," he answered on the second ring, and his voice rang in my ears as cut and dry as ever. I was about to hang up on him, mind you, because that voice of his, so calm and devoid of emotion, intimidated me more than the roar of a lion. However, I had to accept that in counterintelligence, this filthy trade in which I'd been well-trained — precisely by him — *nothing* is what it seems, and perhaps Col. Marlon Berkowitz had powerful reasons for not revealing his move before he played it, not even to me, whom he was obviously using as bait to hunt big game.

"Good afternoon, Colonel. It's me." I breathed.

"Delta!" he exclaimed in what seemed an exaggerated tone of feigned good humor. "Don't tell me you've already started to grow impatient."

I couldn't help a grimace of annoyance. What the hell, he knew me well.

"Maybe I have, sir," I admitted and turned my face to look toward the bedroom where Jessica was still lying on the bed, sleeping, "or are you exercising your psychic powers? There are rumors among the new ones that you can read people's minds."

I heard a broken guttural sound, which could very well have been forced laughter, but he immediately clarified: "Nonsense. It's just that I'm well acquainted with the thorny minds of my most *faithful* servants," he said, emphasizing the word faithful and the expeditious tone with which he answered me brought back my hopes that we were still a team, but I didn't want to get my hopes high, just in case. "Tell me; what are you up to?"

I spoke. "Well, I've had time to reflect on all this and it's only fair that I set things right. After all, it was I who confirmed Pavenko's death in that plane crash, wrongly of course, and the one who failed to eliminate the bastard in New York, when you first ordered his execution."

He was not ready for this, and the hesitant silence that reached me from the other end of the connection made me think I'd caught him by surprise. That improved my mood, considerably; not even the devil is completely infallible, eh.

"Gee, well, I don't know what to say..." he breathed.

"No need to, sir, there's nothing more to talk about, I'm going to settle the scores with old Yuri, and I already know how to do it; I only called you because I need that vehicle I told you about. With any luck, this mission will be closed tonight. Pavenko will not see the light of the next day."

This was pure bravado, of course, there were no guarantees that my plan would work. But it made me feel good to put my boss on the defensive.

"Delta..." he started to speak, but I cut him short.

"Now, look here, Colonel," I said, "I need a compact, fast, maneuverable car and I want some low-caliber handguns with silencers, if you can manage that, concealed in the vehicle's trunk. A shotgun or a submachine will come in handy, too. I need it all here before 11 p.m. Can you get that for us?"

"Of course, I can, but... what are you going to do?"

"I'm going to prowl around Juanchito with Jessica

tonight, Colonel. It's Saturday night, right? I bet I can find Pavenko at one of those disco clubs where they dance salsa. You gave me the idea yourself in the Gendarmerie, remember?" I added, using reverse psychology to make him an accomplice in my coming move. "And, based on my recollections of Operation Red Mushroom, back in Manhattan, plus what I've learned about Pavenko reading his old dossier with the KGB, makes me think I'm going to find him *tonight* in Juanchito, sir. I've got a hunch, Colonel, I'm even willing to bet my precious balls on it! If I fail, you can do whatever you please with me, even throw me to the wolves or to Arnold Feldman's wrath, I don't care, sir. But I'm sure as hell going to try, Col. Berkowitz, sir, with, or without your backing... Preferably with your support, of course." I added, after allowing two seconds to pass.

Apparently, the feigned firmness in my voice convinced him that there was little he could do to stop me. In the end he capitulated, but that didn't mean I was going to let my guard down. I'd seen the old fox being pushed against a hard wall before, and I'd also seen him come back and rip the head off the few who had managed to do this....

"Be careful how you play it, Delta." He warned me grimly. "You won't be able to count on the advantage of surprise. Don't forget he knows you, I doubt very much that he's forgotten the face of a man who almost killed him once; you must think in reverse, damn you, if you were able to recognize him from a photo, despite the time that has elapsed, you can be sure as hell that he'll do the same with you. Pavenko *will* see you coming."

"Precisely, sir. I'm counting on that."

A pause on his end assured me that I had tickled his fancy.

"The truth is, I don't quite follow you," he said, drawing a long breath, "but, I trust you know exactly what you're doing. You always have. Presumably, I'm overlooking something," he added.

He was.

Chapter 10

THE CLUB TERRAZA

It was after midnight when we entered the first salsa club we visited. The place was called the Club Terraza, and it was — according to the information we had — one of the newest and most popular dance halls in all Juanchito, which is why I had chosen it to begin our search. Even though my boss reluctantly authorized our hunting expedition to Cali's kingdom of salsa music, the man insisted on making one condition: Bring an incognito guide with us. Someone trustworthy with sufficient knowledge of the district in case things got complicated and the area had to be abandoned hastily. I reasoned with him that Billings was not acceptable, because he was a gringo cop, in the first place, and if he'd been officially stationed in Cali for five weeks it was likely that he had already been spotted and marked by the opposition. Perhaps Yuri Pavenko had not crossed paths with him yet, being a foreigner, but what about The Scorpion and his gang?

And I remembered then that, back in the 1990s, during the "golden age" of the Rodríguez Orejuela brothers, the Cali Cartel — if memory doesn't fail me — had a certain individual working with them who established and directed one of the most efficient private intelligence services ever known in that part of the world. One that outmaneuvered the Colombian government spooks and even managed to outsmart our DEA guys for a while, until he started getting cornered by his own bosses and decided to turn against them and side with the good guys. His name was Jorge Salcedo — if my memory serves me right — and in addition to being a professional engineer, he'd served as an officer in the Colombian Army Reserve before being a respected businessman and a family man. Mr. Salcedo claims to have joined the Cali Cartel to become the head of security of one of his bosses because he despised the man who was Cali's most fierce rival in the drug trade, the bloodthirsty Pablo Escobar, who led the Medellín Cartel. Some allege that Jorge Salcedo tried to ignore the violence and brutality that surrounded him while he faithfully served the Cali bosses, and that this man struggled to maintain his honesty with great difficulty, until one day he received a commission from his godfather that he could not comply, nor disobey, much less ignore. It was then that he realized that his only escape route was to become a "mole" within the organization and collaborate with the frustrated DEA guys who were striving daily to catch the big bosses of the Cali Cartel and couldn't, precisely because of Salcedo's efficient spy network (they called it the Cali KGB) which was always one step ahead of them in every move they planned. Ultimately, Mr. Salcedo betrayed the richest and most powerful criminal syndicate of all times. If you are wondering why I bring this up, I'll tell you. Taking someone like Agent Billings with us, after being stationed in Cali for five weeks was not acceptable, Billings, being the typical hick cop, was a dead giveaway of who we were and our intentions.

That's how we ended up with a native: César.

Well, he was the ideal candidate among those available, right? Although I still thought that it would have been better for us if we had gone out alone.

I tried to phone Tilson before leaving Las Mercedes, in fact I did, but the man didn't pick up; the mechanical voice of his answering service announced that the user was not available and that if the caller wished, he or she could leave a message at the sound of the tone. I hung up without saying a word and got him off my mind. Now that I had Operation Scorpion Tail back on track, I was going to need all my cranial energy to focus on it.

On the way to Juanchito — Phi and I had settled in the back seat of the car with Mr. Zambrano behind the wheel — I noticed how dazzling Jessica looked on that occasion. The hours of post-coital sleep had done her well and she looked fresh and ready to face anything the night could bring us. She had tied her red hair in a long ponytail which left her graceful white neck and throat exposed, giving her a *very* sexy look. She was wearing a tight black dress, with a short mid-thigh skirt and a low neckline. She had on high heels that, although they would be inappropriate and perhaps even annoying for running, each tip, almost four inches long, would have the same effect on human flesh as that of a sharp stiletto. I'd also dressed in black, with a loose shirt with long sleeves and a Roman collar, my pants were the same color. Although I was not carrying firearms at that time, I had not left behind my Florsheim shoes, with the toes reinforced by sharp steel caps. And a heavy pair of brass knuckles weighed me down in my pants pockets.

When we arrived at the entrance to the Club Terraza, a long line was forming at the door. Two burly bouncers were checking everyone. The men were frisked, but the ladies only had their bags inspected, and not very thoroughly that I could see. I was careful to place the brass knuckles in the back pockets of my pants; I did not believe that any heterosexual Latino male would dare to grope the buttocks of a member of the same sex in public. I passed the inspection because they only frisked me under my armpits and along my flanks until they reached my ankles.

Since we had agreed not to arrive together, César remained waiting for his turn further back in line while Jessica and I walked into the club. I wondered if General Cedeño's man had also seen fit to leave behind the heavy semi auto I'd seen him carrying in a shoulder-holster. I knew that he was a legal representative of the Colombian authorities, and that all he needed to do was flash a Search Bloc I.D. badge to be allowed to pass unbothered, but that sure would mean his end, I reasoned, because if the Club Terraza was owned by The Scorpion or any other member of the Cartel Norte del Valle, *señor* César Zambrano Lora would never make it out of the bloody joint alive. And it was very likely that we wouldn't either.

Two pretty waitresses came out and ushered us with an affable smile on their lips to a little round table for two that, at Jessica's request, was not too far from the dance floor. They seated us and took our order. While Jessica, whose Spanish is as polished as mine, was getting along swimmingly with them, my brain began to sort out the strategy I would use to approach Pavenko, should we run into him that night. By now my mind had stopped pondering what complicated motives existed behind my back for the Colonel to go around blaming me for an "erroneous verification" of Yuri's corpse that had never taken place. What concerned me most now was how to deal with the possibility of being recognized by the Russian arms dealer. Because the bastard would "see me coming," as the Old Man had rightly pointed out. Oh yes, I had no doubts!

As a matter of fact, my strategy for catching him was based precisely on that point. Because everything in life is relative and applicable in reverse, meaning that if comrade Pavenko had changed employers at the end of the Cold War, I might have done it too, don't you think?

That was the basis of my plan.

THE HUNT IS ON
Part Two

82

*C*hapter *11*

SURPRISE

The audience was dense at the Club Terraza that evening — a Saturday night, mind you; your typical night of rumba and party for the Cali youth and for "the young in spirit" who enjoyed dancing salsa and drinking rivers of *aguardiente*, as they say in Colombia, which is almost like saying everybody. People of both sexes and of all ages were crowded there. At 1 a.m. there was no longer room for one more body in the spot and the hi-fi speakers thundered with the flow of that atrocious melody. What can I say, I'm no salsa lover. Young, vibrant bodies jumped around us, writhing dramatically to the frantic rhythm. It was impossible to ignore the superb female physiques, in extremely short dresses as tight as they were, displaying very striking sets of breasts, legs and hindquarters.

I reached into a pocket with my right hand for my cigarettes and lighter, but Jessica, as observant and analytical as ever, warned me about the NO SMOKING signs.

"What did you order, Carrots?" I asked. "*Aguardiente*? That's Schnapps to you. I understand it's the local drink of choice."

"Yes, but I hate it. I prefer Scotch."

"Don't drink whiskey while in Colombia, *chiquita*; it's like going to Mexico to eat pizza and spaghetti. Or order a *taco* in Denmark."

"Yeah, I know. Incidentally, I didn't order whiskey, honey; I ordered us some rum."

The contemptuous tone of her voice made me realize that something was bothering her. And I couldn't help but wonder if it had something to do with the lascivious way I'd been watching those young, female busts and butts cavorting around the dance floor. In the multi-ethnic circles of Greater Miami, I'd heard about how beautiful Cali girls are. Some say it's genetic, and they are certainly among the most beautiful in the world. Maybe it's the mix of races, so common in Colombia, added to the geographic characteristics of the Cauca region. I don't really know. But it is a fact, they are gorgeous, and you will not find them the same in the rest of the country. Perhaps the closest in beauty are the girls from Barranquilla, but those descend from a different indigenous ancestor, whose genes do not mix so well with the Africans when they lack that special touch given to them by a surge of European blood.

"Rum, you say. Hell, that sounds great!" I commented with jovial mischief. "Here comes the waitress..."

The attendant showed us a tray with medium-sized bottles of different commercial brands.

"Which do you prefer?"

"Which do you recommend?" I asked.

"Well, these two are the ones with the highest foreign consumption, *señor*. *Ron Medellín* and *Viejo de Caldas*. Both are of excellent quality, but if you wish to try your luck with the white rum variety, I recommend *Tres Esquinas* or *Ron Blanco*.

I drew a long breath and turned to Jessica: "What do

you think, *querida*?"

"Oh, Pat, I really don't care; take your pick."

"Very well, let it be *Viejo de Caldas*, then."

"*A la orden, caballero.*"

She placed the bottle on the table with two flat cut crystal glasses, an aluminum ice bucket, a bottle of soda and lemon slices; the performance was executed with a certain mastery and a placid smile, after making a graceful bow she left. I read the label that assured the consumer that he or she was drinking a product distilled in the Liquor Factory of Antioquia, 39-proof, stamped with the official seal of the *Industria colombiana*, which guaranteed the product as made in Colombia. A nod of approval, like that of a good wine taster — only this was no wine — and then I poured the drinks. All that was for show, of course; my parents came from Ireland, and as a good Irish pigeon that I am, I also yield my preference to whiskey.

"Here comes our friend César," Phi announced matter-of-factly, "he's walking toward the bar." I waited a couple of seconds to follow him with my eyes, almost relieved to see that the little man had made it inside without making a fuss. I was thinking about this when my partner grumbled: "Oh, God, look who's here!"

Jessica's exclamation had the same effect on me as a stab in the kidney. It hurt. A cold sweat broke out on my body. The matter had to be serious, I reflected grimly, because Phi was not exactly a rookie and she had been well-trained by yours truly to control her reactions. But something unforeseen had happened behind my back that had caused her to break discipline. Something we hadn't counted on....

It couldn't be Pavenko or his partner The Scorpion, of course — we were looking for those two, weren't we? Then, *who* the hell could it be?

I tried to relax, but that wasn't possible; so, I poured more rum into the glass and lifted it to my lips.

*C*hapter *12*

SETBACK

To turn around and look at that precise moment, even though my curiosity had been aroused and I craved it, would have been amateurish. In turn, I bit my lip and held back the urge, of course. Jessica had no obstacles in her field of vision because her chair was facing the entrance of the place, but I had to turn my body one hundred and eighty degrees to be able to watch the newcomer. It took him only a few seconds to cross near our table and I confess that, as I looked at him while passing by, I experienced a real shock. I had not prepared myself mentally for that possibility, and I can't understand why; moreover, in those moments I didn't even remember that the man existed since all my senses were focused on comrade Yuri.

He passed us by without any sign of registering our presence, but he did not fool me. I thought I caught a glimpse of a baleful smile twisting his lips, as if he was thinking *yeah, I screwed up your night.* I looked for Cesar, but I could only see his back as the Colombian agent elbowed his way through the patrons surrounding the bar. *Señor* Zambrano had not yet discovered Mortimer Long's presence and the Moscow Bureau operative rushed to get a table. Feldman's boy wonder was already seated when I finally managed to make eye contact with General Cedeño's man.

"Damn it!" I spat before drawing a sigh. "This is the last thing we needed... How the *fuck* did the dwarf find out we would be visiting this joint, precisely tonight?"

"Seriously, Pat? Do you really want me to answer your question?"

"No! Don't tell me, do you think it was César himself who tipped him off?"

"That's one possibility; there's room for another."

"Oh, yeah? Sure, he could have followed us. All those special agents have the soul of a bloodhound. But the dwarf is better than I thought, I see I made a mistake underestimating him; he's not stupid!"

"Really! And why do you say that honey?

"Don't mess with me, Carrots.... What do you mean, why? He's here, isn't he? He obviously deduced that we know Pavenko better than him, and by simply spying on us we'll lead him to his prey. Plain logic, doll... plain logic."

It was not my intention to unburden myself to her, I must clarify, but I was furious with myself for being so careless. I even remembered that on more than one occasion I'd checked the rearview mirrors to see if we were being followed during the trip to Juanchito, but I never noticed anything suspicious. Now, the question that bothered me was: Had Long *really* followed us? A very dark feeling overpowered me when suddenly I realized that the Old Man had set us up....

How could the Colonel do this to us! I reflected. My boss knew better than anyone else where we were heading that night, he could have passed the information to his superior so that Director Feldman could make his play. It was a way to continue with the farce, supposing it was convenient for him.

"There's another possibility, you know," I said to Jessica, "it could have been the Old Man."

She looked confused. "What are you implying, Pat? Why would the Colonel do such a thing?"

I grimaced. "You heard him, he's being pressured from the top to collaborate with Feldman. Don't forget that he's an expert working at cross purposes and at making ends meet, eh."

She stood silent for a moment, but after a few seconds she nodded her head slowly, then said. "I guess you're right. It could have been him. But let's better focus on the task ahead, for now; Pavenko *must* be found and stopped."

I took a swig of rum and nodded my head. She was right, of course, the Russian was still the main target. However, I found it hard to stop thinking about how screwed we both were in this operation, when our own teammates were starting to worry us *more* than the opposition... Ha!

After sipping a couple more drinks and having a hard time jumping ridiculously on the dance floor (this to maintain our appearance of vacationing gringos) we focused on detecting Yuri's presence amidst the sea of vibrant bodies that surrounded us. But we were out of luck, neither Pavenko nor his new Colombian friend seemed to be at the Club Terraza on that Saturday night. Checking the luminous dial of my watch, I could see that it was already 02:28 hours. I sighed and repressed the urge to light a ciggie, while I poured myself another glass of rum. I tried to meet César's gaze, but the man was not looking in our direction. Long, on the other hand, was watching very intently the female bodies writhing on the dance floor. Apparently, he too was captivated by the beauty of the Cali girls.

The minutes went by with striking slowness, the rum

began to cause its leaden effect and a wave of fatigue ran over me. I stopped drinking. My brain was churning, screaming at me that this was turning out to be a big waste of time. After all, Pavenko probably had more important things to do than killing time in a salsa dance hall... At 03:16 the nausea started again, and I ordered what they call a *tinto* in Cali (a very strong espresso coffee) to fight the sluggishness caused by the excess of alcohol. I was sweating profusely; the heat had become infernal inside the club. At 03:30 I was ready to leave, and I told Jessica so, but the redhead didn't seem to hear me. She didn't even move. Now she was looking carefully at the other end of the dance floor....

There must have been a backdoor, or something, that connected the outside with that section of the premises, because suddenly I had them in view. It was a moment of triumph; I won't deny it. After all, I had bet on the Russian arms dealer and his bloody penchant for Latin music and there he was now: the great Yuri Pavenko, in the flesh! He was walking around with two very Slavic-looking bodyguards, who could very be well part of the special *boyeviks* from the feared Helsinki "Black Army" corps for all I know, being the case that he had now become the Ostrovsky Clan's ambassador in Colombia and was trying to do business with The Scorpion and his gang. They were all sitting around a large table, with three girls and a third party — another enigmatic-looking gent — who was not as big and dangerous-looking like the Caucasian goons but looked to me like that alleged Muslim guerrilla commander we'd seen earlier in the pictures the Colombians had shown us at the Gendarmerie.

"Pat," murmured Jessica, "are you getting the picture? What do you plan to do? I guess you've seen them, haven't you?"

"Sure. I have them in my sights," I replied.

The dilemma that was troubling me came hand in hand with the sudden insecurity that had taken hold of me. Morty Long's presence at the Club Terraza deprived me of my own initiative. *Would the hero from the Moscow Bureau spoil it all for us?* I thought. Well, there was no way of knowing that, but something was going to have to be done about it, and very soon, before Comrade Yuri spotted me among the patrons and took the lead from us.

"I've got an idea, Carrots," I told Jessica. "You just stay put and watch my six, all right? I'll take care of the rest."

Phi started to protest, but it was too late. I suddenly sat up and headed for the men's room.

I'd lied, of course; I still wasn't quite sure how the hell I was going to deal with the problem.

*C*hapter *13*

FIRST CONTACT

Once I entered the bathroom, which fortunately I found empty, I leaned over the sink and taking a worn bar of soap for public use, I washed my hands and face thoroughly. I splashed cold water on my face to clear my head and grabbed a paper towel from the metal dispenser hanging on the wall, then dried myself. The coolness of the water and the smell of soap helped clear my head a bit. I also urinated, marveling at the power and duration of the golden stream with which I drenched the toilet bowl. I flushed it down and put the bird back in its cage, after giving it a good shake and washing my hands again. I moved the brass knuckles to the side pockets of my pants and then tested the spring hidden in the belt buckle, which, when pressed in a certain way, released the set of mini daggers hidden in the leather lining that held the belt. Everything worked like a charm.

Actually, I did know what to do, but there was no guarantee that the ruse would work. Of everything I could think of, though, it was the only promising option. Frowning, I left the bathroom and walked straight to the table occupied by Pavenko and his confreres. He sensed my arrival, as I expected; he was that kind of man. I suppose the Russian was unable to make out my features in the semi-darkness of that section of the club, but it didn't really matter. He was a predator at heart, and behaved like a shark with a built-in organic radar in its snout that can detect approaches by the vibrations emitted by the nearing prey before it enters their limited field of vision. Knowing the flammable element I was dealing with, I was very careful to keep both hands away from my body, where Pavenko and company could see that I was not wielding a weapon.

"Hello, Yuri, how you been?" I spoke. "A little birdie tipped me off that I might find you around these parts, but I was beginning to doubt it. May I sit down?"

The use of his first name stopped the hand that went quickly under the jacket, I guess to draw that black Tula Tokarev he used to carry with him and with which he almost killed agent Landon during Operation Red Mushroom*, back in New York, where I failed to eliminate him. But even though he'd reached for the gun, I didn't think he had recognized me at all, at least not yet, fifteen years had elapsed and time, as we all know, does not pass in vain.

As I slowly approached him, I spoke again with a self-confidence that, if you must know, I was very far from feeling. "What's the matter, Yuri, are you no longer able to recognize an old opponent?"

There was a vacant chair at the table because two of the three girls who were part of their group were sitting on the bodyguards' legs. It was clear to me they were feeling very secure in this place, even relaxed perhaps, they were not expecting trouble. I noticed that the *boyevicks* were engaged in the pleasant task of fondling the women, but my arrival stopped all that, as I became their new focus of attention the two husky Slavs became all business. They even went for their guns.

"Delta?" Pavenko murmured in his unmistakably gruff, modern troglodyte voice. "Is it really you?"

"Well, yes and no," I answered him letting out a sigh. "Le's just say I'm still the same old Coonan. But as for Delta... well, what can I tell you, comrade, that guy was forced into retirement a while ago. Just like it happened with you and all your buddies from the old KGB. Get the picture?"

He nodded and motioned to one of his men, the shorter of the two. The guard broke away from the tart who was entertaining him and came to check me out. He found the brass knuckles and took them away from me, but I wasn't disheartened by that. I'd kept them in my pockets for just that purpose. Finding them would reassure them I was now unarmed. Of course, I could have stopped him permanently had I set my mind to it, there are three responses in the manual to neutralize that move, but I let him do his job without raising any trouble.

"The man is clean," announced the guard in Russian as he stood up and tucked my brass knuckles into his pockets, after briefly displaying them to the boss. The big guy with the square jaw had pulled out a solid short-barreled revolver and was holding it pointed firmly in my direction.

"Can I sit down now, *amigos*? There's no need to attract attention."

"Don't worry about that," Pavenko said, "everyone knows me here. The place belongs to an associate of mine. But sit down, old pal, just refrain from sudden movements and keep your hands flat on the table where my men can see them, okay? I mean if you don't mind."

I grinned and watched him. He had lost some weight, yes, but not as much to become unrecognizable, and a graying goatee made him look a little different than I remembered, but it was him. Oh, yes, the great Yuri Pavenko, the mighty Russian champion of the old KGB!

"Damn," he mumbled once I sat down, "what a surprise to find *you* in Colombia after all these years. The last time I saw you was in New York, remember? You had a silenced pistol in your hands, and you were very focused on putting holes in my skin. In fact, you succeeded!" He roared.

"Ah, that was in the good old days... Everything was so simple, Yuri! We always knew who the enemy was and what should be done to him. But in this new world order...." I shrugged and grimaced.

"You're right, it's crazy. Back then all we had to do was kill each other!"

And as he said this, he put a hand to the lower side of his overgrown abdomen, where the bullets from my gun had wreaked havoc.

"But you cost me twelve feet of large intestine, old bugger, did you know that?"

"Hell, no! I'm very sorry, man. As you rightly said, I only meant to kill you."

Apparently, my witticism amused him because he laughed.

"Seriously, Yuri, that's what my orders specified. You were behaving very badly back in the Big Apple with that team of saboteurs you were leading... What did you expect, man? But that's over now, and water under the bridge does not move any windmills. I'm being honest with you, comrade, the old Delta retired after you hung up your saber. And you can take that to the bank, I don't work for Uncle Sam anymore."

He shook his large golden head in a nod of assent: "Do you happen to like *aguardiente de caña*?"

"Not really, thanks. But I have nothing against a glass of rum. Black rum, *Viejo de Caldas* to be exact."

I did, of course; I didn't want to continue drinking rum, but that didn't fit the image of the new Patrick Coonan I was trying to sell to Pavenko. I took advantage of the arrival of a waiter with the round of drinks and threw a discreet glance around. It was almost 4 a.m. and I expected the place to have cleared up a bit, but it had not. The Club Terraza was still packed with people. I noticed that Phi had left her table to approach the bar, where she sat now next to Zambrano, and the two were chatting as if they were a couple of old acquaintances.

I didn't dare to look around for Long. What was the point? It was best to ignore them all for now and thus prevent Pavenko from discovering that I had secret allies scattered around the place. Although, being a man of his experience, he probably suspected as much....

"Why don't you tell me what brings you to Colombia? Are you still after me?"

I snorted. "In a way yes. But I assure you it's not for settling old scores. Nobody has hired me for that, however... Ah, hell, I don't know if you're going to believe this...."

Raising an eyebrow, he gave me a sly grin.

"Gee, you're not going to tell me you're looking for work, are you?"

"No, man! I *already* have a job, that's the reason why I'm here."

"Seriously? Explain!"

"You see, I work for a very powerful group of radicals. Americans with a lot of money and somewhat different ideas about how things should be run in our country. None of these people agree with the present administration ruling in the White House.

"Right wingers?"

"Exactly! You could say they fall into that category."

"It's a joke, isn't it, you, working for the Ku Klux Klan!

But, somehow, that doesn't surprise me...."

"Hold it right there, partner," I interrupted him, "I never said I was one of them, I'm a mercenary who gets paid for his services, period. And nowadays they are no longer called Ku Klux Klan, just so you know, but White supremacists. They are also called neo-Nazis. You ought to know. Europe is full of them."

"To me they're the *same* shit!" Pavenko spat with contempt.

"True, in principle they are. But this group I represent is somewhat different, they have money, you know, lots, and lots of money, and are much more arrogant than all the others... Do you remember the Castaño brothers?"

This time he stared at me intensely; he'd become very serious, so serious that I was about to think I had pinched a raw nerve, but it was not a good time to hesitate. Had they been clients of his?

"What about them, Coonan?" he grunted, and his expression hardened.

"No big deal, *compadre*," I said in a soothing voice, "it's just for reference. I knew them both and had dealings with them, and if I bring them up now it's because if you knew them too you know very well how powerful these guys were, right? Well, the sons of bitches I work for now are not paramilitaries like Fidel and Carlitos, these are *real* military men! They have people involved in all three branches of the U.S. military, mind you, and there are some powerful politicians also mixed in the pottage. In other words, they are very well backed, Yuri. And they have money to burn!"

"Look, *tovarisch*, I realize this may sound a bit bizarre to you, and I confess that the same happened to me when I contacted them, but the top leadership of this troupe is made up of a bunch of industrial magnates, mostly multi-millionaires, and some career military men. Get the picture? A few of them are already retired, true, but there is a small faction that is not... they are still active within the armed forces of my country, and, as I have already told you, they have rooted themselves deeply in all three branches: the Army, the Navy, and the Air Force. You have *no* idea of what I am talking about!"

Oh, this must have sounded like sweet music to his ears... I saw how his eyes were glimmering, now, but it was not clear to me at the time — Pavenko was a hard man to read — whether the shining in his orbs was caused by greed or rage. He was a man of character as volatile as nitroglycerine; you only had to shake him a little to make him burst... That is why I had to hold on tight to my balls and go on with the lies.

I drew a long breath. "Yuri, none of these skewers is a simple militia man, trust me. I've met sergeant majors, captains, and colonels," I continued to improvise, "and even a fort commander or two in the south of the country, but I'm not going to tell you which... You copy?"

"I hear you. In Russia they also exist, you know, but over there they call themselves patriots and oligarchs. Tell me something, Coonan, do you only work for this group?"

"At the moment, yes; they pay me *very* well and keep me busy."

"I see, but you still haven't told me how I fit into your agenda... And it's about time you do, *amigo*."

"Okay," I said, "fair enough. "Let's get to the point then..."

"Wait a minute, suppose you tell me first what you've been up to these last few years," and as he spoke, he pulled a little fat notebook out of his pocket, followed by an expensive Montblanc pen. Well, he always had a reputation for being a hedonist.

"There was a time, after we were laid off, I was forced to live off my savings. When the dough vanished, I carried out some sporadic assignments for a broker named Donovan, who operated in the New Orleans area. Donovan worked with the American Syndicate, specifically the good old boys from the South. But I ended up selling myself as a bodyguard to the Russian Mafia. I was with Leo Kaminski's gang; I'm sure you can check that out."

"Kaminski, the marijuana planter?"

"Yes; that's what that motherfucker did."

A lupine smile spread his lips. He looked at one of the girls, the most beautiful of the trio, who had remained very quiet sitting next to him. I could tell that she was a good-looking young specimen with a superb female body, in obvious excellent shape, with straight black hair and large almond-shaped eyes that betrayed Mediterranean blood in her, maybe Greek or perhaps Turkish. Who knows. Her expression was sharp, and her black orbs watched me very closely with icy intensity.

"Nina?" Yuri asked without turning to look at her.

"Kaminski is dead, *мастер***," the girl said. "He was killed together with his wife, in Clewiston."

Yuri turned to me and smiled with veiled sarcasm. "Hey, weren't you one of his bodyguards?"

"I was... why."

"Well, what happened?"

"It was I who killed them, Yuri, after they played dirty with me. See, those bastards tried to fuck me over a deal we had, and I didn't fall for it. In retaliation I sequestered the wife and asked the husband for a ransom of one million dollars if he wanted to see her again, alive.

"Interesting. How did Leo react? "He asked without looking at me.

I drew a long breath. "Well, what do you think... The

100

bugger agreed to pay at first, but then he tried to deceive me. He thought that by throwing his best *pistolero* at me he could finish me off. A mountain of flesh and muscle whom he called Goliath...

"Oh, shit! Did you also kill Goliath? Holy Moscow, I can't believe it! And where did all this happen?"

I nodded, looking into his eyes. "Your girl, she said it, this happened in a small town named Clewiston, near Lake Okeechobee, in Florida. But it was nothing personal, Yuri, I swear to God; just business."

He took notes of everything I said in his little fat notebook. "Let's rewind your story a bit to that gent from New Orleans you call Donovan, if you don't mind," he said. "You said this Donovan character represented the American Syndicate, right?"

"Yep, that's what I said."

"What *exactly* did you do for Mr. Donovan?"

"Oh, nothing complex, simple removals. I carried out a few assignments for his clients, he took care of everything except pulling the trigger."

"Your specialty," Yuri asserted.

"That's correct."

"How long did you work with him?"

"Say maybe four or five hits, no more than that. I regretted it when he started assigning me feminine targets. It's not that I have anything against dispatching femmes, but I feel more comfortable blasting away the "heavies". People like you and Goliath, you know, the ones who fight back when push comes to shove. After all, this is how I earn my living and I must uphold my reputation. Plus, Donovan paid less for the women; most of them were minor public figures and hometown politicians."

He grinned. "How interesting, however, friend Delta, I have met some gals who would have given you much more trouble than what I gave you." Here he paused to cast a brief sidelong glance at the Gypsy girl by his side — if that was what she was, she kind of looked like one — but I did not consider his gesture relevant at the time, even though I registered it. It was a mistake on my part, of course, I should have minded it. But I wouldn't realize that until much later. "In any event," he went on, "that's beside the point now. Give me dates, *amigo*, when did you start working for Donovan and when did you leave him?"

"I started with him in '93 and left him the following year."

"And Donovan knew you by your real name?"

"*Nyet*. I worked under an alias: Joseph."

He wrote down the alias too, along with the dates. This guy was very organized, wasn't he?

"And, after Donovan?"

"Then came Kaminski, of course, and *now* I'm with the people I just told you."

He stared at me grimly, as if searching my brain for what I'd left out in the interview. After a moment he cleared his throat loudly and asked: "What are your White supremacists up to? Exactly."

"Initially, they aimed to overthrow the government, but someone in the high command convinced the others that this was not going to be feasible. Then they changed their mind and now they are trying to control the rulers in power to manipulate them. I'm not interested in what they want, Yuri. The pay is all I care about these days, I have to eat, and loyalty to my so-called government employers hasn't got me far, you know. They gave me the boot as soon as my services were no longer needed."

"You didn't understand my question, Coonan, what do they want from *me*? What do they *want*, and what makes you *think* I can get it?"

I didn't hesitate to tell him.

"WMD, of course... *Weapons of Mass Destruction*, get it? They want to purchase Weapons of Mass Destruction from you, and they want them built in Russia or China. Preferably Russian-made. They won't accept anything less, keep that in mind."

I know I was laying it thick. And we were in the most critical phase of the meeting: the negotiation, and don't you think that I hadn't prepared myself for it. I never expected to be able to take him out on our first stumble, there was no way of knowing which way the winds would blow, you know, so, I had convinced my boss to provide me with some bait: ten thousand dollars.

"I can get you anything they want," he said deliberately, after thinking about it, "but, you know, it will cost you. What do you need? Perhaps a nuclear submarine with a crew, missiles and the works, a squadron of Migs armed with smart rockets? A portable atomic bomb? How much money do your people plan to invest?"

"A *lot*, Yuri! Several millions."

Always tell the enemy what they want to hear, is the first thing you learn in the counterintelligence business. The instructors drill it into you from beginning to end, as long as the training phase of your career lasts — and then some.

The Russian mobster smiled almost bitterly, it was obvious, in his behavior, that he still didn't trust me.

"You know, you have no idea how much I would like to believe you, friend; unfortunately, something smells fishy here. However, I do plan to give you the benefit of doubt. I'll give you a chance to prove that you're sincere. *If* you really are authorized by the people you work for to negotiate with me at the highest level, bring me a couple million dollars in cash to open negotiations."

That did catch me off guard; it was like taking a low blow even before the bell rang.

"How the hell do you think I'm going to get a couple of million bucks, in cash, here in Colombia? I don't have a drug cartel boss for a relative, you know! I could arrange a wire transfer to a bank account of your choice with given time... but listen, man, if you really want to do business, you're going to have to..."

"No, Coonan," he stopped me firmly and his face darkened, "*you* listen to me! *You* came knocking on my door, *you*! I owe you absolutely nothing but a handful of bullets in the gut, you copy. If you want to do business, fine, but you're going to have to come up with two million. Without the dough there's no barter, *amigo*."

And then it was my turn to get tough but holding back a bit so as not to lose the prey. "Listen, you fuckin' Cossack," I hissed in a sharp tone, "if you decide to play hardball, I can do it too!"

"I don't give a shit what you do, asshole! Without the millions there's no deal," he growled in that cavernous voice of his. "I'll come back to this joint tomorrow at the same time. If you don't show up with the cash, the doors will be closed to you. This is your only chance, you fool; take it or leave it! And now get out, you Yankee fucker, I've had enough of staring at your ugly snout!"

And with those harsh words he signaled the guy who had confiscated my brass knuckles to give them back to me; this was something I found mighty considerate of him, you know.

I had already given up on them.

---

*Refer to the first book in the series, entitled *The Quadrille* (Author's Note).
**From the Russian language, translated into English as "godfather." (Author's Note)

Chapter 14

THE FARCE

After first contact with Pavenko was made, I didn't want to push my luck that night — God knows that I'd been *very* lucky — so, I exited the Club Terraza as fast as my legs would carry me without attracting unwanted attention. On the way out my eyes met Long's, who was sitting at his table as if nothing had happened; however, there was no sign of Phi or César anywhere. I ran into them outside, later; they were both waiting for me in the car.

"Everything all right, Pat?" inquired Jessica as soon as I settled into the back seat. My partner occupied the front passenger seat, and César Zambrano Lora was behind the wheel.

"Kick it up, César. Get us out of here *pronto*!"

"What?!" he exclaimed. "Are we going to leave Agent Long here, alone?" The Search Bloc agent asked, his black eyes wide with disbelief.

"Mr. Long is a big boy, César, and he sure knows how to take care of himself; besides, he's not a rookie. But the jerk is hell-bent on spoiling the evening for us and I don't want to be around when that happens. I think I've been lucky so far, and I don't intend to push it. Let's split, man!"

He was startled by my outburst, and I understood that it was not to his liking my yelling at him, but he kept his cool. Part of my dilemma, of course, was not knowing what strategy Long would employ. Would he try to arrest Pavenko on his own, or did he intend to rely on our support? Well, it was a stupid question, wasn't it? So far, his reluctance to make eye contact with us seemed to indicate the former.

In any case, there was nothing left to do for us at the Club Terraza. Our objective had been achieved, the bridge to connect with Pavenko was already under construction.

"Listen, César," I told him after thinking about it, "I apologize for getting all worked up, but Agent Long doesn't seem to realize that he's playing with fire, here, or he just doesn't care. That Russian mobster is dynamite, and I know how to weather him without it blowing up in our hands. I can assure you, *amigo*, that Long is no match for this man, and now that we are talking about the king of Rome, can you tell me how the hell he knew where to find us?"

The Search Bloc man maintained his equanimity; his face remained impassive, but the intense flash of his eyes made me think that I had hurt his pride.

"I called him up and informed him that we were coming here tonight," he admitted, "you know, Mr. Coonan, I don't really understand what's going on between you people. How is it that you guys work, huh? I acted under the impression that we are *all* operating as a team!"

"And you are right to assume so, César, of course... although I would've preferred to have left him out of the picture tonight. Don't read me wrong, César, Long is a good agent, but he is kind of young, and somewhat impulsive I am told," I drew a long breath. "I realize this might seem illogical, but Long and Director Feldman are operating from a different perspective than us on this matter."

"Us?" he asked. "Us, *who*?!"

"Uh... I think we'd better leave it at that, for the time being. It will all come clear to you in the end, César, you'll see."

When he left us at the hotel entrance, he was still not convinced of our mental sanity. But we agreed to meet him and his boss again at the National Gendarmerie later in the afternoon.

He drove away in a brooding mood, and we made our way into the room taking all sorts of precautions, as the manual indicated, but no one was lurking behind the door or hiding in the bathroom or the closet. The place was clear. As Jessica closed the door and slid the latch, I punched in the Colonel's phone number. Marlon Berkowitz took the call on the second ring.

"How did it go, Delta?" he asked impatiently.

"Good and bad, sir."

"Explain yourself, please."

"Well, contact was established, and I can almost vouch that there is a possibility we may be able to take him down soon. Tonight was a no-no, though, the circumstances inside the club were not favorable to make the hit. Yuri had a couple of *boyeviks* with him and they were all packing, sir. The Club Terraza, that's the name of the joint where we caught up with him, belongs to The Scorpion, which makes it clear that the advantage was on their side. The place was crawling with Cartel toughies, sir. We could not have escaped alive if we'd tried something."

"I see. However, in the future keep in mind that you

are not paid to escape alive from any mission, Delta, your job is to carry them out."

"Duly noted, sir. Sorry," I muttered humbly into the phone.

"All right, go on."

"Yes, sir. I'm afraid General Cedeño wants to discuss our situation with Long, I understand the Colombians are not clear on how we work these cases. We came across Long at the club, unexpectedly. I presume Mr. Feldman will also be attending this afternoon's meeting and..."

"Oh, no," the Colonel interrupted me, "he's already flown back to Washington on his private jet and left me in charge of the operation. Thank God! We'll just have to deal with Agent Long for the time being. Do you know where that boy is now?"

"No, sir. Phi and I took off from the Club Terraza without speaking a word to him. The guy is a jerk; he never tried to contact us. It's like we didn't exist for him, but I know he saw us. Wonder boy was there to take on the entire Pavenko entourage all by himself..."

"Don't judge him lightly, Delta. I think you are underestimating him. God knows what orders he's been given. I'm sure Director Feldman has his own agenda in this case and Mortimer Long happens to be his best chip on the board... I think Feldman has left the field open to me on purpose."

"How is that, sir?"

"I know him well, he probably wants to be away so that if the mission goes south, he has someone else to blame for it — someone other than himself, or his minions, that is. And since now I'm in charge of the operation, with both you and Phi deployed on the battlefield, the one responsible for any failures will be me."

"Well, I'm not sure you heard me, but I just told you that Long was *there*, sir. He unexpectedly showed up at the Club Terraza..."

"Oh, I heard you all right. I was expecting you to elaborate on that. How did he manage to find out where you were going, anyway? He dared to follow you?"

"Negative, sir. César himself summoned him to attend the party."

"Did Caesar admit to that?"

"Yes, sir, he did, the poor fool is not capable of understanding that, despite appearances, the Moscow Bureau and CI5 do not work well as a team."

"Did you take the time to explain that to him?"

"Not really. I tried to, but I think all I succeeded in doing was to confuse him even more. In any case, the damage is done now, Colonel. We have been summoned to a meeting with General Cedeño himself. I suppose you'll be there too."

"Absolutely," he replied.

I decided then that the time had come to clear the air between us, or at least try to because with this man you never knew. I turned to check if Jessica was still by my side, but just at that moment she vanished through the bathroom door. I waited a few seconds until I heard the shower spray.

"Glad to hear it, sir," I hissed, hardening my voice, "and now that we're on the subject, why don't you come clean with me for once and tell me what the hell you're up to! What do you mean by saying that Pavenko had an accident in Colombia, and it was me, *me* for God's sake, the agent who identified his corpse? You know damn well that never happened!"

*C*hapter *15*

FACE TO FACE

It happened as I expected; Marlon Berkowitz did not answer my question on the phone, after a couple of seconds of constricted silence he ordered me to leave the room and meet him in the hotel lobby. There was a small café where we could talk. He was adamant that he wanted to see only me. Contrary to expectations, Jessica didn't flinch when she heard it from my lips (she had become accustomed to the Old Man's whims, but I suspect she was so tired that she just wanted to go to bed).

Minutes later, when we glared at each other in the hotel's café, I could tell right away that Marlon Berkowitz was not happy with the situation. It showed in the tightness that crisped his features. But in a man like him that was to be expected, and perhaps I'd been a little hasty in forcing my chief to show his hand too early in the game, because if I've learned anything from the Colonel throughout my time working for him in the Quadrille, it's that he always knew what he was doing. Of course, if the objective in this case was to sacrifice me like a goat, I was going to do everything in my power to hinder it.

"You reek of rum," was the first thing he said. "It would have been too much to hope, I suppose," he went on mumbling as we sat down at the table, "that, if only for once in your life, you would give me a vote of confidence... Have I ever let you down, Delta?"

"No, sir," I hastened to answer him in the humblest tone I was able to muster. "But understand, and forgive me, if I remind you that we are going through very difficult times and that we are not, precisely, the most popular branch in the entire OCF. You know that."

"No one better than me!" he hissed in a tone as parsimonious as it was stinging.

A waiter approached us somewhat sheepishly, because, although the man spoke not a lick of English, the fierce tone employed by my boss was so laden with menace that it didn't invite rapprochement.

"Two coffees, please, and make those *tintos*," I said, making use of my Spanish, not precisely the one you hear in Colombia, but the one I often practice with my fellow Latin Americans in Miami, where the Cuban accent predominates.

"*A la orden, caballero*," replied the waiter with much courtesy before gracefully retiring to comply.

The Colonel remained in silence until the two coffees arrived; I held back, it was his turn to speak. When the waiter walked away, the man sitting across from me let out a bitter sigh and tasted a mouthful from his steaming ceramic cup.

"What you are about to hear from my lips is, of course, strictly classified. You will not repeat it to anyone, even if it means your life. Not even to Jessica. Do you copy?

Before answering I held his gaze, so that he would realize that the role of the submissive lamb was already outgrown. From now on, any machinations of his that involved risking my neck would have to be consulted with and approved by *me* first.

I didn't respond verbally, but nodded my head and did so with deliberate slowness.

"Very well. Some years ago, with the rise of Mikhail Gorbachev to leadership in the USSR and the advance of *glasnost* and *perestroika*, I was summoned to a meeting in Washington where I was presented with a very dissimilar problem to the one that the Quadrille had been solving for the nation up to that point. Ronald Reagan, with his Space Defense Initiative program and the creation of a protective blanket in orbit that neutralized the threat of a massive nuclear launch by the Reds, broke the economic infrastructure of the Soviet Union by forcing the Kremlin to invest more and more in the arms race to achieve a technology not yet attainable for them."

"Feldman also attended that meeting," he continued speaking, "and, of course, the man is not as stupid as he sometimes seems, we all agreed that Communism in Russia would soon collapse; as it did. The purpose of the assembly was to map out a strategy for dealing with the new world order that was coming with the arrival of the third millennium. And Feldman, I admit, predicted the rise and expansion of the Russian Mafia across our continent and the infiltration by former KGB agents of the nine clans that had already been active in Eastern Europe, even though the Communist system, closed, tyrannical and anti-capitalist as it is, was not a fertile field for the Mafia to plow. Do you follow me?"

I nodded and went back to sipping from my mug, but I kept my mouth shut.

"Moving forward," he rambled on, "Feldman and I have a history, but it's not necessary to go into the details now, I'll just tell you that our relationship can be as personal as it is professional; that's enough. He resented very much that I was chosen to form and run the Quadrille, because he finds my methods too drastic, immoral, and even harmful to the civil rights of the American people and the Free World, in general. He claims to believe in the concept of justice, that we are all innocent until proven guilty and all that finesse, which is very beautiful and altruistic, I won't deny it, *if* we lived in a perfect world where the real criminals or enemies of our nation and its way of life respected these same principles. We both know that is not the case."

He paused to raise an eyebrow, as if seeking my approval, and I gave it to him with a tacit nod. On that we did agree, indeed.

"But the conversion of former KGB agents and many former high-ranking Soviet military officers into Red *Mafiyia* entities changed the rules of the game and, in Washington's eyes, Feldman's global policing option began to gain ground against my style of shadow warfare, and they made the terrible mistake of cancelling the Quadrille. The Organized Crime Force was created, and Arnold Feldman became its General Director with the considerable backing of the Department of Justice and the Treasury, which, by the way, have defected on the needs of the Department of Defense. New and more liberal airs are blowing today on Capitol Hill with the arrival of a Democrat president to the White House and President Clinton reminds them in a certain way of that young, romantic Jack Kennedy... In short," he drew a long breath, "I have been placed on the backburner. In fact, in certain Washington circles I am accused of being a relic of the Cold War and they even dare to say that my time has passed. How does that grab you?"

"I thought I would be put out to pasture this time," my boss went on, "but I was mistaken. Some senators who are still not entirely convinced that Feldman's methods will work, have decided to keep me around just in case, so they ordered us to infiltrate the East Coast's underworld just to see if it was true that the former KGB inmates would be resurrected with the *Organizatsiya* and so it happened.... When we discovered the presence of Viktor Zotov in Cali, whom you were also supposed to have eliminated along with Pavenko in Manhattan, I suspected that, if Zotov survived your bullets, it would be likely that..."

"Pavenko too," I said, adding a bit of drama.

I thought he was going to call out: *Exactly!* But he didn't. Much more eloquent was his gesture of twisting his lips into a complicit smile and the artful way in which he furrowed his eyebrows. It was as if he were saying: *You are not as dumb as you sometimes look, either.*

"I set out to track him down and found him. Mortimer Long, perhaps unknowingly, was the one who put me on his trail. I learned a lot from the lad by monitoring his elaborate process of tracking and tagging the most prominent members of the Russian Mafia and one fine day I recognized Yuri among the photos in his list."

"I hear you, Colonel. Guess you must have choked on such a bitter spoonful," the embarrassment I experienced when I said this forced me to lower my eyes.

"I did, of course, but I don't know if you'll believe me when I tell you that I also experienced a sense of relief."

"Relief you say, sir? Relief from *what*?! I don't understand..."

He smiled: "I know it's paradoxical but let me reason it out for you. There is no one in the entire OCF who knows Pavenko better than we do, not even Long himself, even though he's managed to tag him and put him back on the spotlight. Long sees him as just a black-market weapons dealer, but you, me, and old Tilson know he's much more than that. He was a nuclear

115

saboteur. His involvement in the Atomic Fang program run by the former KGB makes him more dangerous, his contacts with some highly placed Russian military intelligence chiefs, many of whom are now corrupt, make it feasible for him to smuggle out certain weapons that should be better kept locked up or destroyed to prevent them from falling into the wrong hands.... We all know that what's happening today in the arsenals of the former Soviet Union is a mess!"

"The departure of the Russian Army from Afghanistan uncapped a hornet's nest in the Muslim world and many of those former *mujahideen* fighters trained by the CIA to fight the Soviet occupation have turned against us. Imagine the damage Pavenko can do to us, even unintentionally, just for the sake of profit by setting up a bazaar where any Muslim guerrilla group can purchase weapons of mass destruction..."

"That's as clear as day, Colonel," I interrupted him, "but why did you set up the charade?"

"Because everything in life is relative, Delta, and what sometimes doesn't work one way, works better in reverse. What you must do is find the proper way to turn things around and make them work for your benefit. In short, find a strategic point on which to exert the right pressure, and *voilà*! Get the picture?"

"Nope...." I said and watched him draw a long breath.

"Let me put it this way. Can you imagine how much progress we would make *if* we knew the exact location of that supposed bazaar, when it is established, and we were allowed access to their most relevant clients list? Things would be a lot easier for us, if given the order to eliminate these characters and seize or destroy whatever weapons they acquire while they're being delivered, all in the utmost secrecy, of course... It would be the perfect trap to hunt these darned rats!"

His mischievous grin surfaced again, now he was having fun with me, proving how much farther his neurons could travel than mine.

"The elimination of Yuri Pavenko would only deprive the radicals of their access to the WMDs indeed, but, and we have seen this happen before in the drug market, where there is demand there always are suppliers and soon another one we don't know of will move in to take his place, and another, and another. It would take us a lot of time and effort to identify and tag all the new players in the game. On the other hand, if we take Pavenko and convince him to become our informant and point out to us who his clients are, we can get rid of them discreetly... don't you think we'd get more mileage out of the deal that way, Delta? Sometimes, you must make a pact with the devil to avoid a greater evil."

I thought about it; it was certainly a risky idea if you will, but one with lots of potential; the underground world is full of informants and double agents — even triple ones — so it was not quite a revolutionary strategy but one of utmost functionality.

"Yes, of course," I admitted, "assuming it's feasible. But what can you offer him in exchange for his collaboration? Immunity for all the crimes he has committed against our people?"

"Offer him, you say? I've got *nothing* to give that bastard, other than a good boot in the ass, that is." He paused briefly and grinned wolfishly. "But I can *deprive* him of certain things, well, there's one in particular that this man values the most... And he knows that if I really put my mind to it, I can take it away from him, because he knows us as well as we know him."

At that moment my blood turned cold in my veins; the second I fully grasped what was really going on under the table, and that my legitimate objective in

Santiago de Cali was going to be the total opposite of what I'd been ordered to do here — at least, officially. There was another game being played under the chessboard, one in which Mortimer Long, Jessica Fitts and yours truly were now trapped, and those who were pulling the strings at the top were not the ones who appeared to be doing so at first glance. But there are times in this business when it's not enough just to intuit things and one must press (especially with the type of man I had sitting across me) to clarify the goal of a mission, before taking a step to achieve it.

"What are we *really* doing here, Colonel?" I hissed stiffly. "Would you mind telling me for once?"

His blue eyes sneered at me when he spoke. "What *we* are doing here is not what matters; it's what are *you* going to do? That's the question you must ask yourself. Your real orders, Delta, and get this straight, are very different from everyone else's. Long is going to try to apprehend Pavenko; Phi is going to try to help you eliminate the bastard; but you're not going to do either one or the other."

"Oh, I'm not?!" I spat. "And what the hell am I supposed to do, sir?"

"Quite simple: you're going to fail again, just like it happened during Operation Red Mushroom, back in Manhattan. Pavenko must survive this encounter, Delta, something that — unfortunately — will be impossible for Agent Long. The Scorpion dies, and so does everyone else who crosses your path, including that so-called Muslim guerrilla commander, or whatever he is, if the man rears his head; take them all out, Delta, with one exception: the girl."

Coldly analyzed, it seemed like an impossible mission, but in his mind, it was all perfectly doable, and besides, it was his way of allowing me to make amends for my mistake of so many years ago. *Screw you, asshole*, he seemed to be saying with his smirking look, *if you hadn't screwed up the first time in Manhattan, none of this would be necessary now...*

The fact that I'd been a young assassin trainee of only twenty-four at the time didn't matter to someone like him, of course. Neither did the fact that it had been my very first mission with the Quadrille, and that regardless of my shortcomings I'd managed to keep the Russians from assembling all six components of a portable "dirty bomb" to be detonated on U.S. soil. None of that mattered to old Marlon Berkowitz — hell, no!

But worst of all, I reflected, his reasoning was sound.

Chapter 16

HELL, OR HIGH WATER

I could have asked to whom the Old Man was referring when he mentioned the girl, but I didn't; in some strange way that too was clear to me. He was referring to the young woman with the long, straight black hair, and the large eyes that showed very little emotion. The same girl whom Pavenko had consulted inside the Club Terraza, when he'd been prying into my past dealings with the Kaminski gang.

"Nina..." I muttered and watched his reaction carefully.

The Colonel stared at me dumbfounded for a moment. "And how do you happen to know her name?" he asked stiffly.

Now it was my turn to grin back at him with jovial mischief.

"A little bird told me," I replied with a wink. "Who is Nina, Colonel? What is she to us?"

"Nothing," he said recovering from the shock, "there's the detail; she's important to *him*!"

"To Pavenko?"

"Sure. Nina is his daughter."

Shit! I thought. *His daughter... that's Pavenko's Achilles' heel, the Old Man has threatened to put his baby down if the Russian doesn't give in....*

"I must insist," my boss went on, "that every word that is spoken here stays between us, you copy? Even Phi mustn't find out about this."

"Yes, sir. I understand."

"I'm not worried about you, because I know for a fact that you have no conscience, but a strategy as stark as this may not be well looked at by less experienced agents, so this better be kept under wraps, Delta, do you understand?"

"Yes, sir. I do."

"It's not that I don't trust Phi, you know, but her youth may prove to be an impediment for her to see things the same way I do. Extorting someone, even such a monster like old Yuri, under the threat of taking out his child is not exactly the noblest of tactics in the manual...."

"No, sir. It's a horrible thing to do. But it's effective, right? And the end always justifies the means." I laughed sourly, sometimes it feels great to throw his own words back at him. He ignored my remark, and I drew a long breath. The truth is that in that instant I didn't feel so sure about my so-called lack of morality. But there were other factors at play to be considered and perhaps he noticed in my hesitant tone that even an old dinosaur like yours truly could have some scruples left — even if they weren't many.

"Listen to me, Delta, and listen well," Col. Marlon Berkowitz hissed, "because I am counting on *you* to neutralize this threat. I will not, under any circumstances, allow that scoundrel to go around the world selling weapons of mass destruction with impunity. That is not an option! But if we hit him now, someone else we don't know will take his place and this insanity will go on until one day it gets out of hand and we'll suffer a nuclear attack in our own motherland, because some crazy raghead or other thinks he or she has the right to wipe out our entire Western society. That *will not* happen on my watch!! Come hell or high water, is that clear?" He growled.

That's what it took to get me back on track. To hear in his own words his firm conception and feel the steel of his temperament. When he was so blunt and inflexible, there was no room for any indecisions. In the end, that attitude of his was what always made me swallow all my doubts — when and if I had any. To me he always was our fearless leader, an old lion king, who knew only how to bite at the jugular. That is how I still remember him, standing firm at his battle station despite so many years of service and a goddamned New World Order in which one had to tread very carefully not to lose the balance.

"Are we clear, Delta?" He persisted, misinterpreting my silence for insecurity.

"*Yes, sir!*" I answered right away.

And I did it with unsuspected forceful conviction, in a hard, balls-out manner, holding his gaze just as I had that very first time, when he recruited me for the Quadrille.

After that, Col. Marlon Berkowitz nodded his head and grinned. I knew right there and then he had succeeded in gaining my backing for his cause once more, and I didn't know for sure if that would turn out to be good or bad for me. The memory of Alfred Tilson returned, and more doubts flourished in my mind and heart.

"Is there anything else you wish to ask me?" inquired the old fox, as if he'd read my thoughts. Many believe he can.

"You know damn well I do, sir." I replied.

123

"Well, go ahead, then."

"Who else is aware of what you mean to do with Pavenko, Colonel? Does Tilson know about your little scheme?"

His answer surprised me: "Of course he does, he was the one who gave me the idea in the first place."

Tilson! I thought, and my head started spinning. *So Tilson knew!*

"Don't forget, the man was CIA before I brought him in to train you guys. This is the way they operate, Delta; the Agency is fonder of cunning than brute force because they are in the intelligence business... When I found out that Pavenko survived your bullets, I called up Tilson and let him know. He claimed that if Feldman ever found out that the Quadrille was the one to blame for failing to eliminate him when ordered so, he would never agree to receive me as a sub-section chief in the OCF and we would still be hanging in limbo. So, we fabricated Yuri's death in a fake plane crash, along with all the forged documentation we fed the network files. Tilson himself took care of that; it was he who uploaded the information in our memory banks...."

Well, now everything was starting to come together, but the uncertainty that gnawed at my insides was not exactly a pleasant sensation, mind you. Tilson, that son of a bitch, had betrayed me!

"And you decided to send me to Colombia to verify the dead man's identity, right?"

"That's correct; Tilson made me see that it was the right decision, and he was right. Who better than you, the agent who was tasked with the mission to eliminate him? You'd confronted him in New York, you hunted him down like a wounded animal through the Port of Manhattan, and you *almost* killed him... Who knew the bastard, better than you?"

"You could have used Agent Landon, sir, he was the lead agent in Operation Red Mushroom," I contended, perhaps to see what excuse he would come up with now.

"Landon didn't count anymore, Delta; I had to retire him a few years ago when he was diagnosed with prostate cancer. The right man for the job was you."

Chapter 17

THE HANGOVER

I was able to sleep a little better that night, although I must confess that the unknown, represented by Alfred Tilson's bizarre attitude, continued to pose a dilemma for me. Who was old Al really supporting, was he on God's side or Lucifer's? If he was on his way to betray us, the Colonel must have suspected it. However, my boss had made no allusion to this on our exchange, quite the contrary; he seemed to rely on Tilson's loyalty as he'd always had.

Shit....

I awoke around noon with a feeling that I had not gotten enough sleep. Jessica was already up, and, from my position, I could hear her making noises in the bathroom; she was taking a shower with the door open. I sat up in bed and tried getting up. I didn't succeed. My knees creaked as if my bones were about to tear apart by the effort, thus I fell back on my ass on top of the mattress. It was not one of my best days, that was obvious. Sitting on the edge of the bed I stared in horror at the roll of fat swirling around my waist. I could pinch almost an inch. I tried to push myself up again and this time I put my soul into the act; I did manage to stand up, but a pitiful moan escaped my throat.

"Is that you, honey, finally awake?" Jessica's voice reached me clearly.

"Yes, Carrots, it's me... Jesus, I'm a freaking mess!"

"It's the rum, Pat. You overdid it last night," her voice faded for a few seconds only to come back later, "hey, you want to shower with me? I'll give you a nice massage to revive you."

I considered it for a few moments, as I took uncertain steps toward the window. I pulled back the curtains and could see that it was a rainy day. My whole body ached, especially my joints. It was as if I'd fallen under a furious mule, and it had given me the meanest beating of my forty-odd years.

"I'll be right with you!" I shouted at her on the way to the bathroom, over the noise of the shower spray.

First, I stopped for a few moments at the sink to brush my teeth and then rinse my mouth with a local brand of mouthwash. It tasted minty and helped to freshen up my breath and kill last night's stale rum taste.

"Gosh..." I mumbled to myself, "I feel like shit."

When I stepped into the shower, I found Jessica bending forward with her back to me, she was washing her bushy red mane with scented shampoo, which, according to the bottle, was also half conditioner. Her rearview was splendid and it brought back my lost spirits in one fell swoop. It was a very enticing sight, you know, and I made her aware I found it so by gluing to her body.

"Whoa!" she exclaimed. "The dead are coming back to life!"

"Haven't I told you what an *amazing* ass you have?"

"Me?!" she exclaimed pretending to be naïve, but she pushed her butt against my crotch, arching her back even more to please me.

"Of course it's you, doll, who else?"

"Says the man whose eyes almost popped out of their sockets last night admiring *los culos caleños* in a Juanchito night club."

"Who, me?!" I protested, mimicking her tone.

"Yes, you naughty boy, go ahead and try to play dumb now," she replied, but there was no anger in her words, she was obviously joking.

"You exaggerate, of course, none of those floozies can measure up to you, Carrots." I said as I grabbed her curvy fanny firmly in both hands and gave it all the attention it deserved....

Sometime later, after we had dressed and ordered a hearty breakfast of eggs and steaks, orange juice and coffee from Room Service, we sat at the table on the terrace to ingest our food and watch the rain descend over Santiago de Cali.

"Your knees weren't as screwed up as you claimed", she commented mischievously between mouthfuls, "they didn't even buckle once. Mine did."

"Well, you were the one taking the pounding, Carrots, and I had great inspiration from you, didn't I?" I pointed out with a complicit smile. "That massage...."

"Ah, yes, the massage..." she winked an eye at me and grinned.

The downpour was spreading all over the city and the peculiar aroma of wet pavement, as well as the distant sounds of metropolitan traffic, were part of the atmosphere. I was feeling a lot better now, with a full belly, totally recovered and very comfortable with her company, in the intimacy of the terrace. For a few moments I thought how nice it would be to stay here for the rest of my life, together with Jessica, contemplating the rain pouring all around us. Far from the dangers and vicissitudes that we would encounter when we finally ran into old Yuri-Yuri and his entourage again.

Will we manage to escape alive from this mess? I thought.

There are moments in this business when the mind wanders and one start imagining things... It makes us wish for a different life from the one we lead, a life of which we know very little.

"You're going to kill him tonight, aren't you?" She suddenly inquired. "I mean, the Russian mujik, Pavenko."

"Oh, he is no mujik, trust me, but to answer your question..." I took a sip from my coffee cup, "I haven't really thought about it, yet. But I'm likely to try," I lied looking her in the eye. "The way I see it, he set me up. Once he gets his hands on the money, he'll be the one trying to get rid of us, you'll see. Don't believe for a second that we've deceived him, he *knows* I'm coming for him; Pavenko is not a fool. Even so, I can't let the opportunity pass, it's the only chance I'll get to get close to him."

She sighed. "Yep, I guess that's the trick. I want to be there with you when it happens, Pat; I want to learn more about the Muslim. He interests me."

"Well, don't get your hopes too high, Miss Intelligence Analyst, I'm still not sure the Colonel can get us that couple of million Yuri demanded. Feldman may not approve. If this doesn't work out, we'll have to improvise... I wonder if Long managed to escape alive from Juanchito last night."

"He did. The Colonel phoned early this morning, while you were still asleep. He told me that Feldman's boy was spotted returning to his hotel and, lo and behold, the guy got lucky: he was able to find out where Pavenko and his gorillas are quartered."

Now *that* was some news!

How the hell the Moscow Bureau's man managed to
pull that off was beyond me, but if what Phi was telling me was true, the "little giant" was earning his paycheck.

"Did he really manage that all on his own? Then we underestimated him...." I hissed.

"*You* did," she pointed out, sketching a sour smile that in a way reminded me of our boss, "I realized right away that he wasn't just a brainless body. A lot happened while you were sleeping, Pat. I'm supposed to be the one to fill you in on everything now, since you weren't in a condition to confer with the Old Man when he rang us."

"Well, you're the team's analyst, aren't you?" I interrupted her. "You're the brains, I'm the body."

She drew a long breath and opted to ignore my sarcasm. "Let me warn you," she said, "he wasn't too pleased to find that his most senior agent was snoring his head off and the new girl was awake and ready to receive the information. I know deep down he's a hardcore male chauvinist and prefers you, but...."

"Cut it out, Carrots. Nobody is perfect, and you're taking advantage of my misfortune."

"Not at all, Pat, I'm just warning you in case he brings it to your attention when he sees you. I told him you were under the influence of the alcohol you ingested last night...."

"That should get me off the hook. He complained I reeked of rum when I met him last night, when *you* were in bed sleeping."

"Are you still dizzy, darling?"

"I'm okay, Carrots; talk to me."

"Very well. As soon as we found out where Pavenko is staying, we rented the adjoining rooms next to his suite.

He is quartered at the Hotel Intercontinental; they say it is the best and most luxurious place in the entire city."

"It suits Yuri-Yuri; he's always been a hedonist."

"The hotel is located at Number 2-72 in Avenida Colombiana; that's the exact address. General Cedeño dispatched a team of eavesdropping techs who use DEA equipment to record whatever happens in your Russian friend's room, especially telephone conversations. The problem is that Pavenko is not using the hotel's lines at all."

"That was to be expected," I pointed out, "he'd be a moron if he did."

"He has a satellite phone with him for long distance calls; he has a computer with fax and modem and a cell phone for local calls. General Cedeño's men managed to record what's being said on this side of the world, but we don't know who is at the other end of the line, or what they are saying. Nevertheless, I think it's obvious who they are, don't you?"

"The Ostrovsky brothers," I murmured.

"Exactly."

"Did they get anything relevant?"

"A couple of things. First, we picked up that he's investigating you doggedly. He reported your approach at the Club Terraza to his bosses in Helsinki and, according to the recordings, he seems to be quite excited about the opportunity to become an arms supplier for your imaginary Neo-Nazi group. But he's not acting crazy, I repeat, he's investigating you thoroughly. Contrary to what you think, Pavenko does not expect you to show up tonight at the Club with the two million."

"Really?"

"He was heard to comment that if you showed up with that much money, it'd be too good to be true."

"Wow... I, uh, I didn't think of that. And what does

the Colonel have to say about this? Can he, at least, get me half a million bucks?"

"Absolutely not. A quarter million is all he can procure, for now."

Well, it figured.

Chapter 18

A JUDAS AMONG THE APOSTLES

The meeting at the Gendarmerie had been planned for 22:00 hours. However, at 5 p.m. sharp we received a call from my boss, who told us to be ready as soon as possible; he would pick us up by car. We dressed in formal attire for business: Jessica in a brown skirt and jacket outfit and I in a steel-gray suit. Accompanying old Col. Berkowitz was César (driving the same vehicle that had transported us to the Club Terraza the night before) and we rushed to sit in the back of the car, since the Colonel was in the front passenger seat with the Colombian agent at the wheel. The minute we were settled the Search Bloc man released the brake, and we joined the city traffic.

After a few seconds of tense silence, the Colonel turned his sour face to us and announced:

"We're going to dine out," he said abruptly, but judging by the grimness of his tone of voice, rather than a business dinner with friend César it seemed as if we were all headed to witness an execution in the electric chair.

That made no sense to me, given the fact that we had also agreed to meet Morty Long and General Cedeño at the Gendarmerie later, but I decided to behave myself and not probe indiscreetly. In a few minutes we arrived at Los Girasoles, the chosen restaurant, located north of our hotel on 6th and 35th.

When we were seated at a table, the Colonel spoke: "You may find this little private conference a bit of a shock," we were now on the forty-first floor of one of the tallest and most modern skyscrapers in all of Santiago de Cali, "just like I did when I first learned about it, but I had to agree to it because the idea of this unexpected meeting came from General Cedeño himself and Mr. Zambrano Lora here is only acting as his representative, naturally. So, having clarified the situation for the two of you, let's get on with it," he turned to César before adding: "Shall we?"

"But of course, Colonel," replied *señor* Zambrano.

The Search Bloc man looked a bit nervous. I hadn't noticed it before because, being the driver, he'd had his back to us the entire ride. But now that we had him face to face, his perturbation was quite obvious.

"In all honesty, I don't know how to approach the subject without hurting your sensibilities, but my superior has given me the task and I intend to perform it to the best of my ability. It so happens that... well, there's a very delicate matter that the general has preferred to discuss exclusively with the three of you," he paused to clear his throat. The little man was having a hard time getting to the point.

"Just to be clear," my boss intervened with the purpose of helping him, "when you say 'exclusively,' Mr. Zambrano, it must be inferred that General Cedeño does *not* wish to share this information with the Moscow Bureau agent, correct?

"That is correct, sir," César hastened to answer. "There are some indications that Agent Mortimer Long is playing dirty."

"Ah," the Colonel said.

"Now, wait a minute!" I broke in quite aggressively, and it was something that spurted out of me spontaneously. "Just hold on, man... How can you say, *we think Long is playing dirty*, eh, when last night you admitted telling him where we were heading to look for Pavenko so that he could meet us there, remember? You confessed to that yourself!"

The sharp glance the Colonel gave me didn't say as much as the crooked grin that briefly distorted his lips. Strangely enough, my words had amused him. Of course, César, focused on me as he was, didn't catch it; neither did Phi. But I know my boss well and what his twisted pout said was that he approved of my outburst and my accusatory tone, even if he did not openly admit it.

"That..." stammered César, "that is true. You are right, Agent Coonan, but what I left out then was that I was acting under General Cedeño's orders. It was he who instructed me to warn Long. He thought it would be a good opportunity to observe how the man behaved before you..."

"In other words," I interrupted him, "you wanted to see firsthand if we were in on the take with Long. Right?"

The Colonel suddenly impaled the little Colombian agent with his icy blue gaze: "César?" he asked grimly.

Señor Zambrano nodded his head, looking rather embarrassed, but that didn't stop him from shrugging his shoulders in that specific nonchalant way that only Latinos know how to profess while making it look like a gracious gesture.

"Yes, sir. That's exactly what the General intended," he admitted in a neutral tone. The little man, for all his courtesy, wasn't backing down; but he wasn't pushing it either. Not yet.

"Speak plainly, then. What conclusion have you come to?

"The obvious one, naturally. You are all gathered here with me by order of my general, aren't you? Long has been left out. We believe he's sold out to the enemy..."

"But do you have any proof? Does Director Feldman know about this?" was my boss's next question as Phi remained quieter than a grave; however, her eyes kept jumping from one to the other.

César shook his head before articulating: "No one else have been told, yet."

"When did you begin to suspect Long, César?" I asked.

"Well, let me explain, Agent Coonan," he said while drawing a long breath, "it so happens that we have some very competent elements infiltrating the *Cartel Norte del Valle*. They are first class agents, whose duties are focused on keeping us updated of any changes, or significant events that take place inside the organization, or any new considerable criminal enterprise undertaken by its leadership. What we do know now, for a fact, is that Carlos Rafael Arteaga, The Scorpion, has consolidated his position as the main *patrón*, and that he is in the process of establishing strong business ties with the Russian mafia....

"Our increasing interest in learning more about this dreadful connection with the Russians," he went on, "has our people working overtime and this very afternoon, to be exact, our agents were able to film an unusual scene that confirms our suspicions about Agent Long..."

I could imagine what would follow those words, of course, but it was still somewhat shocking to face reality. I could see myself contemplating it all on a computer screen at the Gendarmerie, as we had previously watched Yuri Pavenko's interview talking business with his Colombian associate.

"What you've just said, Mr. Zambrano, is of great interest to us," the Colonel spoke in a grim tone. "It really is a very touchy subject, as you have rightly mentioned; presuming, of course, that the information is valid. In my long experience in the counter-intelligence business, I have learned not to trust appearances too much; sometimes they can be deceiving. But I do not say this with the intention of questioning your words, which, after all, are nothing more than an echo of what your General Cedeño thinks. I imagine that, at some point, you guys have cross-checked this with the CIA...."

"Forget your CIA, Colonel," interjected César sharply, "we don't want to have anything to do with them. They are not my general's favorite people."

Marlon Berkowitz let out an enigmatic grin before muttering: "A double-edged sword, I presume."

"What's that, sir?" the Colombian asked.

"That it is impossible to overlook that all this could not have happened at a more convenient moment for us, don't you think?"

"Well, yes, sir, if you say so," hesitated César.

In that instant the conversation was interrupted by the waiters, who arrived with our dinner. After they had retired, I took the floor:

"Mortimer Long's case, assuming he has sold out, it must relate to the Russians and not to the Cartel. At least not directly. Whatever exists between them it comes through the bridge with Moscow," I turned to my boss," could you tell me if Morty Long volunteered to participate in this operation?"

It was a mistake, I understood it the minute my boss glared at me.

"I don't know, Agent Coonan. What we're trying to establish here is whether Pavenko's move to buy Long, assuming that's what this is, makes sense or not... And it does, by God that it does! With Long deep in his pocket, he has more room to maneuver."

Of course, that didn't make sense to me, knowing, as I did, that Pavenko was being controlled by my boss. But in César's eyes, and Phi's too, it did make sense — lots of it. What was really brewing here, in Los Girasoles, was the trap that old sly Marlon Berkowitz was setting up for Arnold Feldman and his dashing Moscow Club champion; Long had been chosen to be the fall guy, he would pay with his life for all their sins... Then something inside me revolted when I realized how vulnerable we all are to the machinations of those who command us... we, the nobodies... the soldiers of the underground. Even if he was a complete jerk and would probably never feel anything but contempt for me, his sacrifice was not exactly a trophy I would live to be proud of, now that I knew I was to be the butcher who would slit the lamb's throat.

"Exactly," Jessica concluded, "that's his insurance policy. That's why he travels to Cali and meets with The Scorpion, hierarch of all drug traffickers on the northern Cauca Valley, and that obscure guerrilla commander. Why not do it, right, if he has the *best* protection anybody can buy: that of a U.S. government agent!"

The Colonel's face darkened when he heard Jessica talk like that. His ice-cold eyes impaled her with that tough grim stare that characterized him before speaking: "You are referring to a *corrupt* government agent, Miss Fitts," he corrected her sternly, "let's not mix peaches with apples! But I see your point," he added after a fashion. "What I think is that Yuri Pavenko, or his paymasters in Helsinki, suspected that we were going to intercept them in Colombia and decided to prepare themselves for the crunch. So, do you two agree that Mortimer Long and Yuri Pavenko can be players on the same team?" he asked, staring at us.

"If the evidence proves it," I ventured carefully, "I see no reason to doubt it, sir."

He turned to Jessica when she hesitated and for an unsettling moment, I thought it would all come crashing down on us.

"Agent Fitts?" my boss hissed. "I notice you are hesitating. Do you have a problem with that?"

"It's not that, sir. Accepting that Long is a traitor is not a problem for me. There are traitors everywhere."

"So?" he insisted.

"What worries me is the magnitude of the unearthing. How far does the penetration reach? Does this mean that Mr. Feldman may also be corrupt? And how do we know that Mr. Zambrano, here, hasn't been bought by The Scorpion and his gang? The last time I checked it was still *plomo o plata* in these parts of the continent. Do you know what I mean?"

"Absolutely," punctuated our chief and allowed my partner's words to make a dent in everyone's conscience.

I know sometimes I'm a bit slow, but the further our conversation extended, the better I could perceive the Colonel's Machiavellian mind at work. I didn't have all the details yet, true, but his plan for Operation Scorpion Tail was becoming clearer to me with every ticking second. A thick silence settled among us. I watched as César's large black eyes momentarily dilated and narrowed again. He had great self-control, this little man from the Andes; he swallowed his pride and wiped his mouth with a napkin. He sure was one classy guy.

"Well," he spoke rather gruffly, "*anyone* can be bought, we all know that, but I think we should stay focused on the facts, Miss Fitts. My apologies for saying so but we do have analysts at the Search Bloc too, just like you, and there seems to be a tendency among your peers to over speculate... I strongly suggest we stick to the facts and put all guesswork aside, at least for now. Otherwise, we'll end up losing our minds. I am here with *you*," he said putting his foot down this time, "because General Cedeño, my chief, is very concerned about this situation and he is not quite sure how to deal with it, Col. Berkowitz. He obviously trusts you and your team that is why he is asking for your advice, sir."

Well, I had to hand it to the old fox; I still could not tell how he'd managed it, but things were surely working out for him just the way he'd planned them. Feldman was no longer around to louse things up and Mortimer Long, the only obstacle left in the field to interfere with our purposes, was rapidly becoming a *persona non grata* to the local authorities. Hell, he even had the Colombians coming to *him* for advice now!

"Damn it, César... Your General Cedeño is putting me in one hell of a spot! We all traveled to Cali at his request to assist your people with *your* domestic problems and now you turn around and tell me *we* are the ones with the problems. Gee!"

The Colombian looked down and remained silent. The Colonel let out a long breath before continuing: "However, I cannot ignore this situation. If the evidence you show us is compelling, I will play along with you and the general; we will continue with the charade before Agent Long for as long as it takes my surrogates to wrap up the mission. After that, he is all yours, but not before, are we clear?"

César narrowed his eyes a bit, as if he could see past my boss's charade — and perhaps he could and didn't care so long as we finally got done what we'd come here

142

to do, rid Cali of The Scorpion and the Russian's bad company. After that he did not give us any trouble.

"Yes, sir," he spoke.

"But if it turns out that you people are wrong, and this is a blunder, from this instant I hold you responsible for whatever may happen. Are we clear?" This time Marlon Berkowitz squinted his eyes a grinded his teeth.

"Yes, sir, noted. What you ask is only fair. But it's cool; I guarantee you there is no possible mistake on our part; you will see that for yourself as soon as you watch the film."

And we got to it sometime later, yes, at the *Gendarmería Nacional* before meeting with Long, and everything on the footage seemed to corroborate that the Moscow Bureau's wonder boy was dirty indeed.

But that's the thing about life, isn't it? Always as capricious as a cheap, street-corner whore.

THE TAIL OF THE SCORPION

Part Three

*C*hapter *19*

THE MOMENT OF TRUTH

My wristwatch read one o'clock in the morning when we showed up at Club Terraza; the moment of truth had arrived. Perhaps, in other circumstances, I would have felt the old desire to settle accounts with Yuri once and for all, but — in all honesty — the truth is I was beginning to lose my temper, and it showed.

On this occasion we did not bring César with us. With Feldman gone, my boss gave us permission to move around the city by our own means; he also got us a sports car. However, back at the meeting we had all agreed that the Search Bloc agent would follow us at a safe distance in his giant Ford. General Cedeño had ordered César not to intervene this time, unless it was absolutely necessary, or unless we requested so ourselves. Mortimer Long would also go on his own to prevent the opposition from seeing us arrive together. Not that it mattered at this point, of course, knowing that Long was working with said opposition, but we had to go along with the charade anyway.

Unlike the previous occasion, this time we came armed to the teeth, despite the Club Terraza's strict rules. I was carrying a Ruger LCR .22LR double-action revolver, it was a light weapon with its aluminum frame, also hammerless to avoid getting stuck in your clothes, and like all the magnum cartridges the LR packed greater penetration power than your regular .22 casing. Besides, this little gun held more loads — eight shots in total — than one can expect in any SW or Colt .38 Special. I was carrying the gun in an ankle-holster, and I prayed to God that I wouldn't be forced to dance with the piece wrapped around my ankle. As a contingency weapon, I was packing an AL MAR pocketknife — the Falcon model, if it matters — with a wide, sharp blade that culminated in a well-honed piercing point. Phi was carrying a compact Brazilian semi auto pistol (the Taurus model PT 22) also a .22LR caliber, which was attached to the inside of her left thigh under the skirt with an adhesive band. To top it off, in the trunk of the car, my chief had stocked an Italian-made Franchi Spas shotgun, with lever action and capacity for eight .12-gauge shells in the magazine. A few inches had been sawed off the barrel, a detail that turned it into a weapon for hunting men. All of this came with enough ammo to fight a small war.

We left the car parked half a block away from the premises with all doors locked and the alarm set. We approached the club on foot and found the back entrance. The pair of individuals guarding it were very different from the burly young men who controlled the main entrance. These two grim specimens were creatures of a different nature. Their veiled eyes, which showed no emotion and were always attentive to any movement, gave them away. These were sicarios from the *Cartel Norte del Valle* working for The Scorpion, with orders not to let anyone in who was not properly authorized by the big *patrón*, much less if they were *tombos*, as the lawmen are called down in Colombia. In short: hard and cruel men who lacked mercy, empathy, and most of all tolerance.

In other words, people like me.

They stopped us at gunpoint. In my left hand I carried the attaché case holding the money and I handed it over to the nearest man, with the sneaky intention of occupying his hands and thus making it difficult for him to handle his weapon.

"Here, you take it, *cabrón*," I snapped at the thug in Spanish as soon as Hitman #1 tried to put his hands on me. "I'm looking for the fat Russian, *el ruso gordo,* Yuri Pavenko; he is waiting for us."

The guy looked at the briefcase with some suspicion, but finally received it and opened it a bit to pry in. His beady eyes quickly scanned the interior, delighting in the beautiful green of the U.S. dollars.

"*Qué maricada es esta, papá?*" he asked in slang Colombian Spanish with harsh brusqueness.

"Not your concern, *huevón*; this is for that Russian son of a bitch. Just take the money to Pavenko, *hijueputa*. Do it, you bastard! And, by the way, tell him that the gringo, Coonan, is waiting, *comprende*?" that's not my way of expressing myself, but in Colombia, like everywhere else, tough guys have their own street jargon. I was just keeping up.

However, the guy didn't like the ring of petulance in my voice and even less that I'd ordered him around as if I were his boss, but at that point in time I didn't give a fuck for having hurt his feelings. The man was dead, you dig, he just didn't know it.

His partner, Hitman #2, drew what looked like a squat Ingram Mac-10 9mm submachine gun, one of those they call *moledoras* down there — meatgrinders to you — and pressed it hard against my forehead without getting too close. The weapon had an elongated silencer tube attached that added considerably greater length to its short barrel. I held my temper while both exchanged a knowing look and decided what to do with me; then #1 shrugged his shoulders, showing some resignation. The loudmouth *norteamericano* would have to be kept alive until the boss decided what to do with him and the gorgeous red-haired *señorita* who kept him company. For the moment he would do what the damn gringo asked of him, *sí*? His partner approved, and stayed with us but did not let his guard down.

When the man returned, he was being escorted by one of Pavenko's gorillas, the bigger of the pair. I never knew who that human beast worked for, whether he belonged to the secret corps of overgrown Russian *boyeviks* the Ostrovsky brothers kept stationed like a private army in Helsinki or was simply a bodyguard borrowed from The Scorpion's gang. He had the height of a streetlamp post, a body like the Chinese Wall, and a face so ugly and marked by acne that it was scary. For a moment I debated whether to shoot him on the spot or wait a little till he came closer, because if he was one of Yuri's inner circle guys the move could endanger his relation with the Colonel, but in the end I stuck to following my orders, the one that said: *Pavenko must survive the meeting, Delta, but everyone else dies with the exception of the girl...*

The blond mastodon carried a Makarov semi auto in his right, this was the preferred military side weapon of Soviet Russia, and he kept the barrel of the pistol pointed towards the ground, which I took as a good sign: he did not consider us an enemy yet. However, there was no doubt that he would leave me like a cullender if circumstances demanded it. Except that Phi and I had come prepared to fight this time.

Following our attack plan, my partner dropped her purse on the floor and immediately bent down to pick it up. I caught the move out of the corner of my eye and dug my right hand into the side pocket of my jacket, suddenly drawing the big man's attention.

"Hey!" The guy roared and the Makarov's muzzle came up quickly, aiming at my face. But I already knew what would happen next and I didn't worry about him; he was Phi's problem. Jessica took care of the big man with her deadly little pistol, shooting him twice in the left eye while the white gorilla was still raising his gun at me. The rest was a piece of cake.

With an agile swipe of the hand, I shoved the muzzle of the submachine gun away from my forehead and stabbed Hitman #2 first, while he was still brandishing the sturdy Mac-10. I caught him off-guard because the Colombian *sicario* had been following the action initiated by Phi, so I stabbed him twice in the liver before he realized what had just happened. His colleague jumped at me and managed to knock me down. He wasn't as tall as I, but he was heavier. The son of a bitch was strong as a fighting Miura and he also knew how to brawl, but I had not come to Juanchito that night to match my strength and wrestling skills with any Colombian basher. Hell, no! I simply reached out with my right and sliced his throat open with the pocketknife.

It was all over in a matter of seconds, and we entered the building to find ourselves in what looked like a sort of back room that connected to the kitchen. The musical din emanating from inside had drowned out the ruckus of our little battle, including the two shots fired by Phi — .22 caliber slugs are the least noisy. First, I made sure no one had detected us and then we set about going over the two dead men. We stripped the corpses of their weapons and one by one I dragged them into a pile in a corner, where I covered the bodies with a green checkered vinyl tablecloth that I found folded on top of a shelf.

Then we reviewed the confiscated weapons. I took the Makarov for myself, checked the magazine for loads, which was intact, filled with 9mm cartridges. Jessica took possession of the Mac-10.

"These greasy killers love submachine guns," she commented while removing the magazine to inspect the loads and reinserting it into the weapon. Then she set the fire selector in automatic mode and grinned. "Ready!"

Part of our training has always been, whenever possible, to get rid of the enemy using their very own weapons. We do that to leave no trace of our presence. That's why we took the firearms from the dead thugs even though we were packing our own little arsenal.

Using the inner lining of the tablecloth with which I'd covered the piled corpses, I thoroughly cleaned the blade of the knife and some minor spots of blood that stained the back of my hands. I repeated the procedure with the tips of my shoes. Then I took a good look at Phi to determine if she was in shape to move on with the mission, or if the death of the pockmarked face mammoth had affected her. I was pleased to find she appeared calm and in total control. Reaction to the kill would set in in due time, it always does, but she was holding up marvelously for the time being. Good to know that.

We arrived at the door of an office with letters painted in a metallic gold color, spelling out the word: PRIVADO. I didn't stop to think about it, because if I did I would back down. I just held the Makarov firmly in my right hand as I braced to kick down the door when the flap began to open inwards without allowing me to use force. Pavenko's second gunman suddenly materialized before us. The guy was leaving the office hastily with lots of apprehension showing on his face. I did not give him time to react the minute he saw me. I just raised my pistol and shot him twice in the face. At the impact of the bullets, I added the strength of my muscles and pushed the limp body back into the room. Phi followed me in without hesitation.

It was then that the door slammed shut behind us and a familiar voice boomed in our ears:

"Hi, guys. What took you so long?"

Chapter 20

THE DEVIL IN JUANCHITO

Despite everything, it turned out to be a shock finding him there, standing so proudly behind the great Yuri Pavenko, who was now totally reduced: hands and feet tied to a heavy Louis XV wooden chair. Carlos Rafael Arteaga, *El Alacrán*, was also sitting — although much more comfortable, of course — behind a fine wooden desk in front of them. He was playing listlessly with a massive pistol that he held in both hands. The semi-auto bore great resemblance to one of those new heavy Magnum models that the Israelis call Desert Eagle, perhaps it was a new upgraded prototype.

I had to struggle to keep my sanity, you know; the images my brain was taking in now did not agree with the information I'd been fed earlier. Everything was going out of context and the scenario that Col. Berkowitz had painted for me at Las Mercedes was rapidly vanishing in the mists to give way to another reality... a *very* different one.

How come — I asked myself — after having been told that Mortimer Long had sold out to the enemy and having seen with my own eyes a classified video of the Moscow Bureau agent conferring with the head of the *Cartel Norte del Valle*, that this new circumstance had come to be?! A situation in which he seemed to have achieved the original goal of our joint mission all on his own?! Had Long already captured the Russian arms dealer?

God, this isn't happening, I thought in disbelief, *and why the hell does The Scorpion look so cheerful, now that his "nuclear tail" has been cut off...?*

My head began to spin; this was insane. I saw the same confusion appear on my partner's face, although she could not even remotely imagine *everything* I knew!

I turned my face toward Long, who was smiling slyly as he pressed the muzzle of a 9mm Glock at the temple of a defeated-looking and battered up Yuri Pavenko. The Russian weapons dealer's cheekbones were swollen to the point of disfigurement and his bushy graying hair was disheveled. I also noticed someone had placed the briefcase with the quarter million on Arteaga's desk, and that in another Louis XV style chair sat that mysterious gent — whom the Colonel believed was a Muslim guerrilla commander — and that Nina, the girl I was not supposed to hurt, was conspicuous by her absence....

While I was trying to make sense of it all, Jessica reacted as she had been trained to by aiming the business end of her Mac-10 at The Scorpion and his massive pistol.

"Drop the weapon, Don Carlos!" she snapped. And the harshness in her voice made me accept once and for all that things were not what they seemed.

"Don't shoot, Agent Fitts!" Long bellowed. "The gun isn't loaded, I checked it out myself!" He took a step toward Jessica. "It's just a purchase sample that Pavenko brought for the boss."

It was difficult to focus on what was evolving around me, I don't deny it, because nothing was happening as we'd anticipated... Arteaga should have been dead by now, as well as Mortimer Long and the swarthy-looking bearded fellow who was keeping them company, Commander Ahmed, but in some strange way that had me puzzled I couldn't bring myself to pull the trigger. Phi and I were paralyzed! A whole range of ins and outs now hovered above us.

However, there was one key question that increased its stature in relation to all others: *Why was Pavenko being arrested in the very presence of the man we all believed to be his business associate and protector, in Colombia?*

What the heck is going on...?!

And those queries were joined by others, naturally: *Why did the almighty Scorpion appear so cheerful, sitting in the unusual company of a bad ass gringo cop and a presumedly dangerous Muslim guerrilla?*

Where was the rest of his in-house security force? Furthermore: *If Morty Long had sold out to the Ostrovsky Clan, why instead of siding with them did he have Pavenko beaten to a pulp and tied down to a chair while holding him at gunpoint?*

"Disarm him," I ordered Jessica, pointing my chin out at *El Alacrán*, "but do it carefully, will you?"

She didn't hesitate to act on my order, although it was obvious that Phi remained confused, or at least as confused as I was. I waited with the Makarov firmly grasped in my hand, aimed at an intermediate point between Long, Pavenko and the silent Muslim.

Surprisingly, Arteaga did not resist; with a gracious gesture he took the gun by the barrel and extended the handle to Phi in an act of submissive surrender. But he did it graciously, mind you, because he was a really classy gent, a Latin Roger Moore of sorts — if I may say so. The most curious thing about the man was that he did not show a gram of apprehension about our invading presence in his sanctuary. He kept a floppy facial countenance, touched by the hint of a disdainful grin, as if he were a superior being from another planet, or something, in the presence of lesser creatures. He was dressed in an Italian-cut light linen suit, a brown silk shirt with a Roman collar that gave him a somewhat ecclesiastical appearance. I noticed that his hands were rather large and powerful, like a bricklayer's or an industrial mechanic's.

There was a very unpleasant aura hovering around this man, something intangible that reached your brain in waves, alerting the body's defensive sensors about an ominous sensation of impending danger, like when you step right into an ambush; I'm not sure I can explain this well. It was like entering a cave you believe to be vacant and gradually coming to terms with the fact that, hey, guess what, you are not alone! No doubts about it, this Scorpion character certainly was an overwhelming psychic force, whose body language resembled that of a giant green Anaconda, those overgrown bone-crushing snakes that dwell deep in the Amazon jungles. I could see impending death reflected in his mean reptilian eyes....

Grinning an evil smirk that was both dicey and hypnotic, The Scorpion lay slumped in the expensive Louis XV chair behind a splendid wooden desk, contemplating our movements with languid interest and in the most absolute silence.

Once Jessica had confiscated the gun, Arteaga remained very still, probably thinking about what he was going to do with the two gringo interlopers, while he watched us intensely with those ophidian eyes of his. Since it was becoming obvious that Long did not intend to kill us for now, I decided to give my undivided attention to *El Alacrán*, but not before passing a signal to Phi to keep a watchful eye on the bearded Muslim.

"Very well, *señor* Arteaga," I said, now facing the highest authority of the *Cartel Norte del Valle*, with the nozzle of the Makarov pointing at the carpeted floor. "What are we supposed to do with you?"

The condescending smile that stretched his lips widened; I think he was expecting a similar reaction from me.

"It is not me you need to get rid of, Mr. Coonan... I am just a local *traqueto*, remember? An opportunist, if you will, who struggles to stay at the helm of this vast criminal organization everyone in Cali refers to as the North Valley Cartel. Well, that's the impression I work hard to project. Fortunately, General Cedeño believes that." Let me emphasize that the English in which the man addressed me was impeccable, it even retained a resilient British accent that was shocking to hear in one of the most un-British looking fellows I'd ever seen. Despite being a Colombian mobster, Arteaga's careful pronunciation and refined demeanor was that of a well-educated gentleman from the old school, who had nothing to envy to any member of the British higher classes.

English lord, my ass! I thought.

"Your command of the English language," I murmured, unable to help myself, "is amazing... Wow, where did you learn to talk like that?"

"Oxford, of course," his smile expanded, "I was raised and went to school in England," he confessed with somewhat veiled pride.

I drew a long breath and spoke.

"That's awesome, *señor*. Let's see what we have here then. An American agent who is supposed to be corrupt, or so I'm told; a Weapons of Mass Destruction dealer who is hooked up with the Russian Mafia; a new and aggressive leader of the *Cartel Norte del Valle* whom the Search Bloc people describe as the king of the *traquetos* and — correct me if I'm wrong, Your Highness — a guerrilla commander of the Muslim faith... Right?"

Long burst into laughter upon hearing that. He sniggered heartily for quite some time, although he never relaxed his watchful attitude toward Yuri. Then he turned to the bearded gent and said: "Did you hear that, Ahmed?

The Mohammedan warrior nodded but made no further comment. This man, contrary to Arteaga and Long, seemed worried and extremely tense. Apparently, my presence in the room made him nervous. I can't say I blame him for that, though, there's a good many people around the world who have the same reaction when they get to see me at work.

"It seems," said Long, "that all the ingredients for a good spy thriller are gathered here, don't you agree?"

"That's right," I conceded, "but who dares to tell me the rest of the plot? I can't wait to see how it all ends."

"Be patient, Coonan. Maybe Don Carlos will feel encouraged to do it," Long suggested. "In fact, I would do it myself, if I could, but forgive me for not daring to divert my full attention from Comrade Yuri, here."

He was right to think so; Pavenko was not the type of enemy that could be neglected in custody; he might be older and badly beaten now, but he was still a dangerous and resourceful opponent to deal with.

"Why not shoot him in the head and end this madness once and for all, Agent Long," this was Phi speaking now. "Isn't that what we all came here for?"

He kept his eyes on her while struggling to hide his contempt, as if she were not a beautiful professional woman with enough wit to read between the lines. His face was contorted with the effort he was making not to release all his fury on us, but I still couldn't understand why Morty Long felt that way, since he seemed to be the one holding the upper hand.

"Yes, of course. That would be the easiest, right? It's probably what your devious chief has ordered *you* to do. You damn murderers, that's what you are! You're all a disgrace to American law enforcement, you... You have *no* idea what it has cost me to get this far..."

Arteaga stopped him by raising a placating hand, because he sensed that if Long continued down that path, things would get complicated for them.

"That's enough, Mortimer, don't let these two get on your nerves, lad."

"But..."

"Enough," he said rather stiffly, "do yourself a favor and let me take it from here. You told Coonan that I would be the one to explain everything, very well then, let me do just that. Your duty is to focus on this one," and he turned to point a thick brown index finger at Pavenko. "You know the grand scheme of things better than anybody, Mortimer, and the pieces are already falling into place; this is *not* the time to lose your temper, don't you know?"

Long shook his head in exasperation, but after a couple of secs he finally drew a long breath and gave in to the well-modulated voice of this extraordinary creature. "Okay, okay, Don Carlos... you win. I have no patience left to deal with this fool!"

The 'fool', of course, was *moi*.

The Scorpion smoothed his long, ocher-tinted kinky hair and nodded his head slightly before addressing me: "Now, Mr. Coonan, we are on the verge of finally achieving what no one has been able to do before in the entire history of the American intelligence community: centralize and coordinate the covert operations of *all* our security agencies!"

Although what Arteaga was saying was of great interest, no doubt about that, the best part of my attention was still focused on the man from the Moscow Bureau. I was extremely concerned about his obvious discomfort with our presence, and though Long kept struggling to maintain control of his actions, it was becoming increasingly obvious that the "crazy horse" — as my boss had once called him — was about to flip and start kicking out savagely. It was only a matter of time. But he was not my only problem, I too was carefully watching Commander Ahmed, since it still wasn't clear what role he played in this new bizarre tripartite coalition. The Muslim was also beginning to worry me, as he sneaked venomous sidelong glances at my partner Phi, while she kept them covered with her squat Ingram SMG and the sturdy SIONICS noise suppressor.

The thing is that all the farce was unnecessary, and I had no valid reason for prolonging it. In fact, I was violating my orders with every second that the three characters surrounding us remained alive! My clock was ticking, and time was running out... Jessica noticed it in my eyes. If I had not yet blasted them all to hell, it was because of the curiosity Arteaga's little speech about centralizing power had aroused in me. I sensed that something *big* was cooking behind these three flunkies; something that Col. Berkowitz *needed* to know.

"I warn you, Don Carlos, that I am not very patient either, just like this *fool* here," I said pointing at Long with the muzzle of my Makarov, "if you have something to tell me, do it bluntly, my dear man."

I realized he did not take well to be warned, I should have known that, but it was already too late for any regrets. The Scorpion fixed his sly reptilian eyes on mine, making me feel the power emanating from his brain, an overwhelming force launched at me like a torrent of live energy to melt down my already over-heated neurons. Oh, that *hijo de puta* was totally out of the ordinary! I had never faced anyone like him before! This business is full of rude, implacable men, but this snaky motherfucker possessed a rare quality of deadly subtlety, which was something newfangled to me.

So much like Sax Rhomer's Fu Manchu, I thought.

"The United States of America, *our* country, and I say ours because, believe it or not, I *am* an American citizen, born in New York, is about to enter a new world war, not in the classic sense of the word, but a holy war against the Islamic people and the Muslim world... A crusade if you prefer."

As he kept on talking, I reflected that the shitty Muslim extremists were taking center stage again, even though we had all traveled to Colombia to hunt down Russian mobsters and the new, more violent breed of drug barons called *traquetos*. For a moment I seemed to be listening to my boss, when he'd briefed me at Las Mercedes about hypothetical Weapons of Mass Destruction bazaars and mixed guerrilla groups with sufficient funding to invest in atomic and biochemical weapons. A true house of horrors!

"Here we have Commander Ahmed," he said and pointed to the owner of the name with his index, "a CIA *sleeper* planted deep in a guerrilla cell led by Osama bin Laden. Have you heard of him?"

"Nope," I confessed, "no idea who the guy is."

Long gasped at this and opened his eyes wide. "Jesus!" He snapped. "Didn't I tell you that this guy is an idiot?"

"But she *does* know, doesn't she?" Arteaga ignored Long and turned to Phi. "Do you, Miss Fitts?"

Jessica smiled at them without losing sight of Ahmed,

163

who was not comfortable at all with the revelations Don Carlos was making about him. "It's possible," she replied with some humor.

"The CIA trained Bin Laden well in Afghanistan; we taught him everything he knows today and threw him at the Russians so he could practice his terror tactics with the Soviets. Once the Red Army fled Afghanistan, the elongated bastard turned on us and has been screwing up our lives with his surprise attacks ever since. But what happens to a madman like him without a supplier to sell him weapons? He becomes a nobody, right? Or a mad dog without teeth. And we hurried to cut off the umbilical cord that supplied him, that is until this piece of *crap* that you see here came back from the past!"

To emphasize The Scorpion's last words, and perhaps to vent his own rage, Long slammed the butt of his Glock into Yuri's mouth. The blow cost the Russian a bloody mouthful of teeth. Pavenko grunted and groaned before crying out loud in pain and helplessness, and somewhere in that room — I swear to God — *something* unseen stirred... But it was only for an instant and since everything remained the same, I thought that if the devil had condemned what my countrymen were doing to his disciple, the time had not yet come for the master to rise from hell and stand beside him.

"We, I mean the CIA, have an unorthodox way of working these cases, a way that has earned us the despise of some high-ranking officers among the Colombian security agencies. General Cedeño, for instance, he is one of them. It seems the Search Bloc bunch gets along better with the FBI and the DEA, but since the Feds are not authorized to set foot outside the country, for the moment at least, the Colombian authorities are forced to work with the OCF... that is why Mr. Long is here."

"Really, Don Carlos? Did you say *we* have?" I emphasized the word we.

"That's what I said, Mr. Coonan. Believe it or not, I'm a CIA Non-official Cover, a NOC, if we use the correct Langley terminology. But no one here knows that, not even the DEA. And it *must* remain that way, old sport, they are not supposed to find out."

If that were the case, I couldn't help thinking, then why the hell was he telling *me* for?

Well, I didn't like the obvious answer.

"Between Commander Ahmed and his people working out of the Middle East," he went on, "and I with the assistance of Agent Long on this side of the continent and in Eastern Europe, we have managed to identify the most notorious arms dealers who emerged from the ruins of the Soviet Empire. There is a secret list at Langley which contains all their names and whereabouts. There are *ten* individuals in total, Mr. Coonan. Ten, and Yuri Pavenko is one of them."

"Not anymore, eh!" spat Long. "He's going to rot in jail!"

"Yes, that he will," agreed The Scorpion, "but not in a federal penitentiary as is the norm with the big Mafia dons back home, the CIA is building a secret prison in Guantanamo, a gigantic and impregnable complex where all these rats are heading. There will be no trials, Mr. Coonan, no human rights will be respected or protected by the U.S. courts of law; we are going to torture them both mentally and physically, until they give us every bit of information that we need to put an end to these deadly souks they are setting up in different regions of the world. Oh, yes, we are going to give these buggers a taste of their own bitter medicine."

And that was the very first time in my life that I heard anyone talk about the terrible Strawberry Fields, a clandestine prison that would eventually become "the terror of all terrorists," if you pardon the redundancy, although at that point in time, it had not become a well-known name yet.

"You sons of bitches want to blow up government buildings in the States and destroy our embassies overseas, huh?!" Long growled and hit Yuri again, very hard, but this time he did it with a fist, not the barrel of his Glock. "Well, you're about to get fucked, you fat bastard, get your ass ready!"

Pavenko roared again in plain powerlessness, and this time he began to spit around and curse out loud in his native tongue. The Russian arms dealer seemed to have gone mad, his eyes sparkled like those of a furious fire-breathing dragon in the darkness of a dungeon and that unfathomable anger for which some of his compatriots are famous in Russian history (including Ivan the Terrible and good old Josef Stalin himself) took over him. He struggled to break the bonds that tied him to the chair. And, again, I felt — only stronger this time — that inexplicable sensation that *something*, or some-one, was disturbed by the hurt of the beast in some dark corner of The Scorpion's office... The hairs on the back of my neck stood up — and let it be known that I'm not in the least superstitious — when the devil finally raised from Hell and bellowed: *Here I come!*

Chapter 21

THE GRAND FINALE

There are moments in life, especially in circumstances like this when events do precipitate, that being a good mentalist helps you freeze time in one's imagination to study the details of the incident more closely. But, of course, that is only possible to achieve in the mind; in real time nothing can slow it down. So you can better understand what I am trying to explain, imagine that the events I'm about to narrate unfold in slow motion....

A shot (can't tell where it comes from) echoes off the walls of Arteaga's office, and I feel the painful impact of a medium caliber slug smash against the twenty-seven layers of Kevlar body-armor that hold my bulletproof vest.

Once violence breaks out, Phi's training forces her to react, again, by taking out the closest target she has in sight, in this case Arteaga, despite the story we'd just heard, and Jessica aims her Mac-10 at him.

"What are you doing, you stupid bitch?!" *Long bellows, an expression of disbelief distorting his features as he turns to aim his Glock at Jessica.*

"Careful, Phi!" *I hear myself cry out before I shoot Long twice in the chest, but another shot rings out again and this time I feel a hot botfly buzz off very close to my neck.*

Stunned by the shot, I turn my head in time to see the heavy curtain that covers the back wall, behind the chair occupied by Ahmed, collapse with a loud crash as it falls over Jessica and her submachine gun while she struggles to keep her balance. Another shot rings out and suddenly I have before my eyes the same young woman with jet-black hair, huge eyes, and buxom breasts with the face of an innocent she-devil, who was sharing the table with Yuri and his bodyguards during our first meeting. It's right then and there that I realize that she has been crouching behind the curtains all along, waiting for the right moment to join the party. Or perhaps she has delayed her intervention to listen to what Arteaga and Long have revealed to us, and we, subjugated by the peculiar circumstances of the moment, never detected her presence.

"Kill them all, Nina!" *Yuri shouts with passion.* "Shoot these bastards!" *And this is the first time I face the fiendish aim of that dangerous young lady, whom I would later know as Nina the Gunslinger.*

In a hasty attempt to describe her (and I say hasty due to the nature of the circumstances in which I find myself), I could do so by saying that she is dressed all in black with high boots and a combat jumpsuit, made of elastic fabric that hangs tight to the body, like a second skin, a garment that highlights her divine figure and that incredible pair of breasts that a low neckline allows me to admire, as she contorts her torso while taking the hard blowbacks of the rapid-firing Uzi SMG she is holding in both hands. She is also wearing a pair of dark glasses that covers her dead killer-eyes and gives her an impersonal appearance, like a female facsimile of the Terminator from the movies, an automaton programmed exclusively to kill! Kill! Kill! In-

168

stead of a human who reasons and feels.

The girl does not waste time, she turns to attack Phi and puts her out of action in a flash with a butt to the head; but as I endeavor to pull Jessica out of her way, she aims her UZI at me again.

I know I can kill her, but my orders are precisely the opposite, even though Yuri appears to be defecating on his deal with my boss by ordering his daughter to take us all down. Her next shot whizzes by only a few inches from my head because fractions of a second earlier, sensing her move, I throw myself face down on the floor and roll on the carpet until I find reasonable cover behind Arteaga's solid wood desk. The Scorpion loses his composure before the unexpected appearance of the gorgeous she-devil who is now bent on getting rid of me and, in a mechanical reaction, he pounces on Long's corpse to seize the fallen Glock. He is grimly determined to defend himself with the fallen OCF agent's gun, so I turn to face him raising the Makarov and, from my position on the floor, I shoot him twice in the head.

Yuri watches everything from his position and it is then that he assimilates that I am on his side and that (despite appearances) the Colonel is keeping his side of the bargain; had it been any other way, Nina (and he) would both have been already dead by my hand.

The young woman also senses what's happening and turns to glance at her mentor, as if waiting for a counterorder.

"That's enough, baby!" he shouts, raising his arms. "Forget those two, for God's sake! Help me get free and let's get the hell out before it's too late!"

I feel the disturbance that the girl causes in the process of freeing her father, but I don't dare to leave the cover of The Scorpion's massive desk, not yet, or *show my head above its burnished surface. Tempers are running high tonight, and it is better not to present an easy target, just in case....*

When the calm reigned inside the office, I risked peeking over the desk with the Makarov ready to blast away in all directions at the slightest indication of trouble. But there was no need to, Nina and Yuri had totally vanished.

Only the dead, us, and the infallible smell of blood, smoke and gunpowder filled the room. The bearded Muslim warrior we now knew as Commander Ahmed, and the briefcase with the quarter million dollars, were also gone.

*E*pilogue

Two days after the closing of Operation Scorpion Tail, with its results uploaded by my boss to CI5's online archive, we found ourselves back in the modern building that housed our headquarters in Midtown Miami.

The Colonel gave us a fervent rebuke for "having allowed the Russian arms dealer to get away" (this was for show in front of Phi, of course) but what seemed to really bother him was the escape of the Muslim guerrilla, when Jessica told him he is known as Commander Ahmed and that he was a CIA plant within a terrorist cell operating in the Middle East led by one Osama Bin Laden.

I remember the frown that Jessica's words brought to his face and how he pricked up his ears, like a hunting mastiff does when scanning the horizon he catches the scent of prey. It was right then that I sensed that despite everything we had achieved, *something* must have gone wrong, and it didn't take me long to see it had.

When I was alone with him in his office, after he crisply ordered Jessica to go meet with Mrs. Aledo, our chief of staff, and find all the information she could gather on this Commander Ahmed and the Osama bin Laden fellow, in addition to look for any operation that the CIA was carrying out in Colombia, the Middle East,

Helsinki, or even Moscow — for God's sake! — the man started venting with me.

His first reaction was to punch the surface of his desk, something that really impressed me because he was always a man with a strong disposition, very well-tempered nerves, and very prone to controlling his emotions. But everything that was related to the OCF, and/or its director general, Mr. Arnold Feldman, made him lose his cool. Of course, there was another angle that also bothered him deeply: the intervention of the CIA in an area that crossed our jurisdiction, although it was understandable that the boys from Langley, whose theater of operations is the entire world with the only exception of the national territory, were after Pavenko's tracks once he conceived the "brilliant idea" of getting rich selling Weapons of Mass Destruction to people like this Bin Laden fellow and his band of Islamic terrorists.

Yeah... That sure as hell made sense!

When my boss came to his senses — it didn't take him long, mind you — he picked up the receiver of his multi-line table phone and made several calls. When he finished the task, he raised his edacious eyes from the phone and fixed them on me with the same fierceness with which the Spanish *banderilleros* stick their spikes into the charging bull in a *corrida*.

"This is unheard of, Delta," he hissed, "didn't I tell you to get rid of *everyone* except the girl and her father?"

"Yes, Colonel, you sure did, and believe me, I *tried*, but Phi turned in a report on the events that took place in Juanchito, and you must admit, sir, that the picture that was presented to us in Arteaga's office was very different from the one you sketched for me... Don't you agree?

"Well, yes; that's true..." he admitted reluctantly. "It never occurred to me that the bastards from the Moscow Bureau were doing the same thing as us but by other means and with an unsuspected ally: the CIA, for God's sake!"

"What irritates me the most," he rambled on, "is that Langley did not warn *me*. Why the hell do you think they acted that way, huh? We've always done each other favors, in fact, when Tilson screwed up on a mission in Moscow during the Cold War, I offered to receive him and give him a job with the Quadrille because his Section Chief, Martin Stevenson, did not want to make a Roman circus with him or put a price on his head so that they would silence him away from home, although he was forced to lay him off...."

He stopped because of the intensity of the look I threw him. Quite a meaningful stare, I must add.

"What?" he snapped.

"I wonder what the hell is going with Alfred Tilson, Colonel, where do you have him working now?"

Will you believe me if I tell you that he didn't answer my question? He remained silent while staring at the ceiling of his office, absorbed in his own reflections, but it didn't take long before he bid farewell to me with a half-hearted wave of his hand without further ado.

I could tell he was not satisfied with the results we had accomplished in Santiago de Cali.

I won't lie to you, sensing his unhappiness with the outcome of Operation Scorpion Tail gave me a lot to think about and nothing of what went through my mind was good, I tell you. But you learn to roll with the punches, and it was certainly his turn to worry now about the political backstabbing Washington is famous for, that was his theater of operations and his responsibility, as mine was to deal with the tactical problems that arise in the field. But when I arrived at the files room looking for Phi, Mrs. Aledo confronted me and told me in her rather smug tone that from that very moment, according to the Colonel's orders, we were both granted leave and since, neither Phi nor I had anything else to do there, we might as well get lost until further notice.

Minutes later, as I was about to leave the building, Jessica intercepted me in the hallway that linked her office to mine and motioned for me to accompany her into her quarters. Puzzled by her scheming attitude, I reluctantly agreed, even though I was already burning to get away, and we locked ourselves together in her office.

The light on the flat screen of her computer was on and when she told me to pull up a chair next to hers at the computer terminal, my eyes came across a still image of that beautiful Russian she-devil that almost took my life, down in Colombia.

"I know who that girl is, Pat!" my partner breathed passionately. I've already mentioned that Jessica is a very competitive woman, and the trap that Nina had set up for her, not to mention the kicks on the ribs and the blow to her head, had turned the young Russian into a hated rival of hers.

"What are you talking about, Carrots? Let's get out of here. Hasn't Mrs. Aledo told you that the Colonel has approved R & R leave for both of us?

"Yes, she did, but first I want you to see this... That gal who saved Pavenko's fat ass back there in Juanchito is a rarity!"

I drew a long breath. "Phi," I said in a placating tone, "you shouldn't take it personally. We are all vulnerable at one time or another, and there is always someone better..."

"No *fuckin'* way, Pat! She's not better than me! But she is *very* dangerous... That bitch is a poisonous snake of the worst kind! She looked so young and innocent back there, at the Club Terraza, that I never imagined that... Anyway, you shut up and listen because this won't be the last time we will cross swords with Nina Tetriak on the field. Oh, no! Didn't the boss tell you?"

"What? Nobody ever tells me anything around here..." I mumbled.

She ignored my feeble attempt to play her issues down and rambled on. "The Old Man has placed Yuri Pavenko at the top of the Elimination List and that Nina Tetriak works with the Russian arms dealer."

"Nina *who*? Okay, Carrots, who the hell is she?"

"She was a child prodigy in a circus act in Moscow. It has been a challenge, but I have managed to find out all about that woman, never mind how, the story goes like this: Yuri Pavenko met her when she was only five years old, during a visit to the Gypsy Circus. The origin of the relationship these two birds of prey share has nothing to do with physical attraction, since Nina was an infant when Yuri saw her for the first time. What caught his attention about the Gypsy girl was her pistol skills..."

"Come on, Carrots! Pistol skills, you say. Who the hell can aim a pistol right at only five years old? You are nuts!"

"As soon as he saw her shoot in her circus act," she went on sternly, "Pavenko sensed that cultivating her with love and patience would be of significant use to him. Protected by the privileges granted to him by his position within the old KGB, Yuri managed to tear Nina away from her family and forcibly adopt her. He took her to live with him, he taught her to kill in cold blood and over time, by pampering and pleasing her every whim, he managed to make the girl come to admire him and see in him a paternalistic figure. Of course, none of this stopped the bastard from making her his concubine when she blossomed onto such a beautiful young woman...."

She paused deliberately to stare at me, and I caught a playful glint in her eyes. "You're probably aware of that unhealthy and inexplicable attraction that some young women feel for men that are almost twice their age," she added.

"Don't go there, Carrots!" I replied to her malicious hint. "I'm not that ancient, damn it!"

Jessica laughed at my reaction, which had been carefully designed to lighten up her mood, even though it was to be done at my expense. Actually, if one compared her twenty-something years to my early forties, she was right: I could very well be her father.

"What do you think of the story, eh?" She asked, suddenly becoming serious.

"Wow... It's a fable. The ogre who falls in love with a gorgeous princess."

"Make no mistake, Pat," she stopped me instantly with an apprehensive look, "*she* is the ogre, Nina the Gunslinger, that is what they called her in the Circus and later, when Pavenko joined the Ostrovsky Clan, she also gained fame in Helsinki's underworld using that same sobriquet: Nina the Gunslinger..." she repeated, spacing out the syllables to emphasize their meaning. "Her reputation as a paid executioner precedes her everywhere she travels. She is a professional assassin!

"The beauty and the beast," I commented, somewhat distracted.

"Yeah," she said. "Like you and me."

I was wondering if my boss was aware of this. According to what the Old Man had told me in Colombia, he believed the girl was Yuri's daughter. But if she wasn't, and Jessica was right in what she had dug, then the Achilles' heel that Marlon Berkowitz thought Pavenko had was no such thing. Of course, there are many mature men who fall madly in love with younger women for whom they are capable of risking even their own lives; boy, don't I know it.

"Have you informed the Colonel about this, Jessica?"

"Not yet. Maybe I'll do it when we return, maybe not... I know he doesn't like me sticking my nose where I'm not told to and what he ordered me outright was to investigate any joint operations between the CIA and the OCF in which the Russian Mafia is involved. But since I've I been told that they have granted us both leave," she said while mischievously grinning and winking at me, "to hell with everything else... Let's split!"

After stopping at my 3/2 L-shaped abode in Miami Springs to pick up some useful things for a road trip to sunny Naples, we loaded everything into the trunk of the vehicle the agency had assigned me for personal transportation — a late-model Jeep Cherokee Classic — and headed toward the beaches of the West Coast, on the central part of the state.

Driving pleasantly through the I-75 toward the Gulf of Mexico, I felt much better as we began to leave behind the suburbs of Broward County and so many ugly memories associated with Operation Scorpion Tail, back in Colombia.

It was a splendid sunny afternoon that invited people on leave to enjoy the summer and the beach life of South Florida. With a languid knowing glance Jessica and I promised ourselves not to discuss any more work-related topics in the coming days; we promised each other every gesture, every caress, every thought...

And we fulfilled it.

THE END

ABOUT THE AUTHOR

OSCAR ORTIZ was born in 1959 (Matanzas, Cuba), but he was raised in the United States. From an early age he showed a talent for art and literature and (to the same extent) his dislike for collective sports, business, science, and math. He spent his youth studying commercial art & advertising. Ortiz is the winner of the "Sole Second Prize" in the **2006 ENRIQUE LABRADOR RUIZ INTERNATIONAL STORY-WRITERS AWARD** with his crime story *La culpa fue de Hammett* ("Blame it on Hammett") and was selected as a finalist in the **2006 TELEMUNDO WRITERS WORKSHOP** contest. He has worked as a freelance screenwriter for Telemundo Puerto Rico and Cubana de Televisión Studios in Miami. He currently resides with his wife in South Florida.